BEETHOVEN AMONG THE COWS

Rukun Advani studied English Literature at St Stephen's College, Delhi. His Cambridge Ph.D. on E.M. Forster was published in 1985. He works in the editorial department of Oxford University Press, New Delhi.

Happy 60'e

love

xxx x.

BEETHOVEN
AMONG THE COWS

Rukun Advani

faber and faber

LONDON · BOSTON

First published in 1994
by Faber and Faber Limited
3 Queen Square London WC1N 3AU

Phototypeset in Palatino by Intype, London

Printed in England by Clays Ltd, St Ives Plc

© Rukun Advani, 1994

Rukun Advani is hereby identified as author of this work
in accordance with Section 77 of the Copyright,
Designs and Patents Act 1988

A CIP record for this book is
available from the British Library

ISBN 0–571–17044–7

For Bitia and Kéya

Contents

Acknowledgements

I began writing because of Shalini and Chitra. In print, it is only possible to thank them. To Sonoo and Ann I am wordlessly grateful for love and support at crucial times, and poached eggs in between. Kéya, Bitia, Rahul, Ania, Suvir, and my parents have been emotional anchors without strings.

The literary approval of Dr Brijraj Singh, Mukul Kesavan and Robert McCrum has mattered enormously. Dr Brijraj made the linguistic possibilities of English literature percolate into many unsuspecting bloodstreams; he has a *moral* right to half my royalties. Mukul's conversational articulation, witty iconoclasm, and devastating bluntness with all forms of writing that he considers long on words and short on inspiration have helped me as much as his generous-spirited criticisms of specific phrases and passages. Robert's succinct and clear-sighted opinions have been invaluable; without his regular encouragement I could not have shaped my sketches into this novel.

My fellow editors at Oxford University Press have been close friends and given shape to thoughts, prose, and much else besides: Esha, Ivan, Roslyn, Anomita.

Ratan and R.K., Shikha and Jayashree, Martin and Jane, Chris and Billie, Rajeev and Tani, Neel and Chitra, Rana and Ben, Ram and Sujata, A. Shahid, Arvind M., R.P.J., R.D., Sikha, Sunita, Sanjeev S., and Reka and Hartej have been extremely generous with friendship, interest and encouragement. Mr and Mrs Shetty have been wonderful guardians.

Earlier versions of chapters 3, 5 and 7 were published in *First Fictions 11* (London: Faber, 1992); an earlier version of chapter 4 appeared in *Katha Prize Stories II* (Delhi: Katha/Rupa, 1992).

I was the world in which I walked, and what I saw
Or heard or felt came not but from myself;
And there I found myself more truly and more strange.

– Wallace Stevens, 'Tea at the Palaz of Hoon'

1

Nehru's Children

Sarojini Naidu probed me as to why I cared for
Nehru so much. I said 'He calls out my maternal
instincts.' She was very struck by this. She said, 'He
does that with the whole of India.'
                              – Edward Thompson, quoted in E.P. Thompson,
                                              Writing by Candlelight

At the midnight hour, when clock hands joined palms in respect-
ful namasté and India was born, my brother and I weren't even
twinkles in our father's eye, perhaps not even specks in his pool
of protoplasm. We arrived some time later, both on afternoons of
different years, when clock hands looked more like the splayed
legs of a woman, pushing out two brothers reluctant to come to
terms with real life. Being thus bundled out to face facts, we lived
as active orifices in the daze of infancy, mewling and puking our
way towards consciousness and clear sight until, one day, the
blankness froze into winter and a milk-white cow which jelled in
the frost came calling on us every morning. She arrived like a
ritual at seven-thirty sharp, punctual as an alarm clock. It was the
year the Chinese invaded India, a little before Nehru died of a
broken heart.

Each morning that misty December, when a fog of ashen pallor
clung to the road like the ghost of an albino and the Chinese
bayonets got closer and closer, that cow ambled out of a Vedic
haze to wake us up for school. We lay curled inside a womb of

quilts. Each day we felt afresh the birthpangs of a cold delivery as Amma cried out like a Hindu muezzin:

'Wake up boys, Mrs Gupta is here for her breakfast.'

The cow got her name from her lookalike, our neighbour. She was fat and couple-coloured, a wheatish complexion fading towards patches of white leucoderma, just like Mrs Gayatri Gupta nearby. They were both placid ruminants with spindly legs and they chewed just like each other, with the same slow muscular motion of their jowls. When my brother grew old enough to draw, his first sketch was a Picasso. It showed a quadruped with a tail which resembled a monstera plant, numerous udders shaped like fjords in some Scandinavian belly, and a human face forcibly transplanted into the general region of a cow. Underneath his first masterpiece my brother was more considerate than any Cubist. He wrote: 'Misiz Gupta is my favrit animal.' Meanwhile I, the older of us two, supplemented his small step towards Surrealism with my own giant leap towards lunacy:

> I saw a cow
> It was playing with a sow
> And do you know
> Just now
> It jumped over the moon, and how!

Each morning that winter, with our school closed and fear of shortages in the air, we fed Mrs Gupta a daily newspaper. My brother and I would rush out to the balcony where she stood, waiting to be made an offering. Abba, who subscribed to newspapers from every corner of the country, would stack away most of them and hand us one.

'What's this?' I asked him the first day he gave me a newspaper.

'Give it to the cow,' he said grinning, 'maybe she'll eat it.'

She did. The paper was called *The Hindu*.

That first day when I shredded the paper and Mrs Gupta chewed it up with those measured, thoughtful, neighbourly movements of her mouth, Abba laughed so hard that I was alarmed and thought the cow was about to die. My brother didn't know whether to be alarmed or laugh, and after looking dubiously between us for a moment, decided it was more politic to follow his father. He began laughing slowly at first, to suggest there was reason for his merriment which no one should doubt, then advanced by well-considered stages to an unnatural pitch of mirth. I stayed neutral for a while but then the infection strung my face out into a smile and soon, though I did not know why, the three of us were shrieking all over the balcony, pointing at the cow.

Mrs Gupta gazed back at us with no effrontery or malice. She chewed stolidly, her legs did not buckle. After our laughter slowed down to grins we fed her more newsprint.

'Scrambled, boiled, omelette, fried or poached,' yelled Amma from somewhere behind. 'Which do you want for breakfast?'

'*Reader's Digest*, quick,' shouted Abba, 'I want a *Reader's Digest*.'

There was a strangulated silence, followed by the muffled sound of Desdemona being stifled. 'What?' she managed to cry out, before appearing in her nightie like Juliet on the balcony.

Amma had a Shakespearean range of facial expressions which derived from the arts of Europe – a Beethoven frown, a Mona Lisa serenity, a Rubens cherubism after lunch, a Jeeves-Wodehouse arching of her eyebrows, a Nelson's eye when the occasion required and a Medusa glare which turned servants to stone. You could absorb Western culture just looking at her. That morning, stopped short by Mrs Gupta, she first took on the visage of Queen Victoria on a bad day, frosty and imperial, but then she saw the joke and brought us natural fodder. The cow consumed several issues of *Reader's Digest* without trace of humour. Then she ate many plastic bags with the same thoughtful relish. Some old record covers of 78 r.p.m. disks absorbed her equally: Mrs Gupta cleaned out the façades of Beethoven's 'Emperor' Concerto and the Amen Chorus of Handel's *Messiah* as easily as certain anti-Communist propaganda couplets which were shot through with Nehru's Shelleyan idealism on the socialist Brotherhood of Man. The couplets asked the Chinese leaders to shake hands with

Nehru, eat chowmein with him, and generally come to their senses:

> Jaisé doodh aur malai
> Hindi-Chini bhai bhai.
> Hosh mé ao, hosh mé ao
> Chou, Mao, hosh mé ao.
>
> Jaisé noodle, vaisé pulao
> Nehru saath chowmein khao.
> Chou, Mao, hosh mé ao
> Hosh mé ao aur chowmein khao.
>
> Haath milao, gaal milao
> Nehru saath haath milao.
> Chou, Mao, hosh mé ao
> Hosh mé ao aur haath milao.
>
> Dono bhai Chou, Mao
> Nehru saath baith jao.
> Baith jao aur chowmein khao
> Chou, Mao, hosh mé ao.

That cow swallowed everything. She was a religious animal whose digestive tract transcended communism, culture, conflict and the cold of that bitter winter which ate into our bones like the austere logic of a Jack London story. I suppose I might have saved a lot of *Hindus* by denying her, but in that gloomy season when we were too young to understand the meaning of war but old enough to catch the scent of danger, that oblation to a holy animal kept the climate of the times and our subconscious fear of invasion at bay. In an age enveloped by a vast mist of insecurities it gave us the illusion of power: we felt as potent as Romans handing out Christians to the lions.

When that *Hindu*-chewing cow walked into our lives, Abba decided to dig up every little scrap of writing, zoological, scientific or literary, that might register somewhere in our minds and

4

make us moral. Two fragments which connected with Mrs Gupta settled in our heads as comfortably as Abba sinking into his evening armchair, reading to us while my brother and I grappled with his shoelaces and Amma hovered happily nearby.

'Listen to this,' he said, soon after the Chinese invaded Ladakh and stopped forever there, drawing a permanent boundary line at the point where they felt their force quail before the incredible colour of the Pangong Lake –

> 'The cow is of the bovine ilk
> One end is moo, the other, milk.'

– and we thought that summed it up very well.

But that wasn't it: on the other side of the cow lay the world she had shut out for us. An army general and several brigadiers were taken prisoner, the rhetorical flourishes of the dark god from the rain forests of the south who ruled the Defence Ministry foundered as underclad men were sent off to fight in the snow, our vocabulary swelled with chilblains and frostbite, and all the while, over many mornings, Mrs Gupta ate newsprint which showed Nehru walking through roses with John F. Kennedy, she bit implacably through Marilyn Monroe and Jackie Kennedy, she had her fill of Dev Anand and Sophia Loren, she converted Cassius Clay and Mohammad Ali into equal doses of the same white milk, she mooed in harmony with Elvis Presley and Joan Baez, she chewed the cud over pictures of Mao Tse-tung and Chou En-lai who had betrayed their friend, Nehru.

On another evening, clutching a scrap of paper, Abba summoned us again: 'Just listen to this, just listen to this masterpiece by a clerk who is now the poet laureate of our Defence Ministry.' He read out the scrap, and this time Amma doubled up so hard with laughter that my brother and I looked at each other with unanimous alarm:

The Cow is a wonderful animal, also he is quadruped and because he is female, he give milk, but he will do so only when

5

he is got child. He is same like God, sacred to Hindus and useful to man. But he has got four legs together. Two are forwards and two are afterwards.

His whole body can be utilized for use. More as the milk. What can it do? Various ghee, butter, cream, curd, why, and the condensed milk and so forth. Also he is useful to cobler, watermans and mankinds generally.

His motion is slow only because he is of amplitudinious species. Also his other motion is much useful to trees, plants as well as making flat cakes in hand are drying in the sun. Cow is the only animal that extricates his feeding after eating. Then afterward she chew with his teeth – whom are situated in the inside of the mouth. He is incessantly in the meadows on the grass.

His only attacking and defending organ is the horn, specially so when he is got child. This is done by lowing his head whereby he causes the weapons to be paralleled to the ground of the earth and instantly proceed with great velocity forwards.

He has got tail also, but not like similar animals. It has hairs on the other end of the other side. This is done to frighten away the flies which alight on his bottom body whereupon he gives hit with it.

The palms of his feet are soft unto the touch. So the grasses heads would not get crushed. At night time he poses by lying down on the ground and he shouts his eyes like his relatives, the horse does not do so.

This is the cow.

We really came to life that winter when the air, so thick with Nehru, condensed into a cow. We understood the importance of digesting words to make our language pure and fluid and saw why Mrs Gupta was venerated. She helped us overcome the Chinese invasion during the days when the enemy came near but were stopped in their tracks by the Buddhist trance of a navy-blue lake. Through the undercurrents of our fear and between foggy, forbidding horizons, she cut through the threat of newsprint and provided us conceptual salvation against that cold coming.

Gradually, other holy beings started coming to light within the shrouds of that same early pea-souper which clothed Mrs Gupta's approach to our home and the Chinese decline at the Pangong Lake.

By the time we arrived in the world the real Gandhi, the original, bald, bespectacled, emaciated saint who spun out the very fabric of our nation, had left for his heavenly abode where we presumed he sat crosslegged with a charkha for halo, spinning khadi to convert God against the Lancashire cotton of all the British angels who held a monopoly over Him. On the arid earth below my brother and I knew him mostly as a man of large ears and a toothless, affectionate smile from the obligatory sepia picture which beamed down from a central height in the school assembly hall. Each year a couple of schoolboys were deputed to clean out the cobwebs which accumulated behind that picture and garland it in readiness for the commemoration prayers of 30th January, Martyr's Day, and one year that task fell to my brother and me. A master-on-duty, the Black Panther, in whose Anglo-Indian mind affection mingled amiably with abuse, growled in our ear: 'You two over there, d'yoll see that picture up there? That's the Father of our Nation m'boys, and he needs a clean. Yoll get some clean dusters and dust him out carefully an' all. And mind yoll don't break the bloody picture men.'

'Yessir, yessir,' we mumbled, rushing off for dusters and a ladder.

When we took the picture down the Panther snarled: 'O bledgy hell men, what's this an' all?' His close inspection revealed that a combination of silverfish and damp had eaten a bit of the martyr's chin and were fanning up to take his mouth. The Panther snatched the picture off us to alert the principal, who said they had better get a new picture for the Martyr's Day garlanding ritual. He had a dictator's moustache which issued instructions into a phone: a new picture of Gandhi was ordered. But the replacement which arrived was a much smaller photo: the picture company said it no longer did large Gandhis. Might the school be interested in a large Nehru instead?

Our principal, a retired colonel of correct demeanour, was eclectically in tune with Nehru's industrial plans, the Sandhurst philosophy of General Ayub Khan, the cultivation of rose gardens, and gastronomic well being. He recognized at once that asceticism and cheap cotton were things of the past and assented to the laws of the market. A diminished martyr came up at a lower height on one side of the hall, and pride of place was given over to Gandhi's heir – him who interrupted our lives one hot summer evening.

'Chacha Nehru is dead, Chacha Nehru is dead!' cried Kéya Gupta from her balcony to our small group on an improvised cricket pitch on the road in front of our houses.

'Shut up Kéya,' I said, then turned to the others: 'Wait, wait, hold on, not so fast, carry on bowling, she's talking rubbish, it's my batting time, I'm not out.'

I was in my nineties, needing the last few runs to hit my maiden century in our one-man-batting single-wicket no-back-runs one-tip-catch-out tennis-ball-cricket game. Ramesh and Pramesh, Intelligent and Skylab, Mohan and Salim, David and Farookh, all put their hands on their hips. They looked ready to call off the game at this opportune calamity.

'Chacha? Chacha Who?' asked Ramesh. His politics was weak but he could make his piss come out in two streams, one vertically down, the other horizontally forward. He was an idler whose primary interest lay in the aesthetics of excretion, whereas his twin Pramesh was the most agile fielder of our group. Pramesh could scatter the stumps from any angle, as sharp as Rusi Surti or Colin Bland. I never dared attempt a run when I hit the ball anywhere in his direction; whereas with Ramesh, who spent all his spare time scratching himself and scrutinizing the parts he had

8

scratched, I never needed to be wary. 'Whose Chacha is dead?' he demanded, coming in from silly point.

'Shut up Kéya,' I yelled, walking fiercely towards the balcony with my bat raised to dispel the certitude of her broadcast.

Farookh Modi, whose mother was an anaesthetist and who normally went to sleep keeping wicket, whipped off the bails the moment I left the crease.

'Out,' he screamed with uncharacteristic vigour, 'out, out!'

'Wait a minute, what d'you mean out? If Chacha Nehru is dead, the ball is dead, that's the rule,' I said weakly, 'but he's not dead and I'm not out.'

Everyone came in crowding to gang up against me.

'Bhai what is this, bhai what is this, new-rule shew-rule and all?' said Farookh aggressively. 'In which cricket rule-book is written ball is dead if prime minister is dead?'

'So what d'you think you're bloody Farokh Engineer or what?' I yelled back, invoking the national wicketkeeper's name in vain.

'Yoll men shut up an' all, I say,' said Intelligent, who had been nicknamed so because his voice boomed out like a double bass and gave weight to his words. He went to our Anglo-Indian school and rhetorical questions were his forté: 'Don't yoll know if Pandit Nehru is no more we can't play an' all men?'

'Yes, now we can't play an' all men,' agreed Skylab Singh, who always toed his brother's line. His hair was knotted up into a little bun from which wisps sprouted, looking like jagged antennae from a satellite. He had been born the day an American skylab was predicted to fall from its orbit onto Indian soil. In the event it fell in North Canada, twenty years later.

'Yes but, yes but,' said Salim Dewan, the youngest, coming in from third man. Salim lived in a state of existential quandary and liked to field in the margins of every game, far from the madding crowd's ignoble strife. In a fit of Nehruvian secularism his Hindu parents had named him after the fourth Mughal emperor, though that might equally have been because Salim's father drank as heavily as the late Mughal, or because Salim himself early evinced

9

a similar proclivity. 'Yes but now we should be silent for two minutes,' he said. 'After that I have to drink my milk. We can play after minimum two minutes. Just now is drinks interval.'

'We have to respect the departed leader,' said Mohan scratching his crotch, 'and also I think my papa is calling.'

'Shut up Mohan, your papa isn't back. You only want to fly your bloody kite and just because now it's your fielding time you want to stop playing.'

I said this in a general tone meant for everyone, looking threateningly at Mohan. Despite being born on the 2nd of October, same as Mohandas Karamchand Gandhi, he was always experimenting with untruth. There was no possibility of his wanting to go home; on the contrary the entire endeavour of Mohan's life was to fly kites and stay clear of his father, a bad-tempered botanist who claimed he had a Ph.D. from Japan and who crowded his verandah with potted bonsai plants. Mohan's mother stared at the plants in dismay all day, and her attitude to foliage seemed symptomatic of the state of their marriage. I was never sure whether the plants in Mohan's verandah were short because his father had a Japanese doctorate or because they shrank a little every day from his mother's basilisk gaze. By evening Mohan's mother, dulled by her day-long contemplation of verdure and worn through by the small-town monotony of a returning husband, sighed wearily like Tennyson's Mariana and watered the plants to keep the roots of her marriage from wilting. Within Mohan, his parents' tensions caused evasion to become a way of life and kites an obsession. He was averse to cricket but ran hell for leather after cut kites to capture them as they fell, repairing the rents in them with glue of an orgasmic consistency. He bought kites from wooden-shuttered shops which perched over open drains where the urine had turned grey with age, he collected kites painted the colour of forty-seven national flags, and he flew all his kites with myriad-minded singularity. He was a tricky spin bowler who hated fielding. I knew he was itching to go kite-flying and glared at him as viciously as I could.

'Hey Kéya,' I said to the little girl on the balcony, 'who told you all these lies about Chacha Nehru. He was fine yesterday. Didn't you see his photo in the *National Herald*?'

A row of sceptical faces turned in unison at the little girl who stood like a cold, dispassionate umpire on the balcony.

'My mama heard in the radio,' said Kéya. 'Now he's dead.'

'Will you shut up and go away,' I roared. 'You're not allowed to stand so close to the balcony like that. He's alive I tell you. His picture was in the paper yesterday an' all men,' I said, feigning intelligence.

'*National Herald* is owned by Pandit Nehru,' said David Arren, whose father was a bald journalist in the rival daily, *The Pioneer*. 'In *National Herald* they have to show Nehruji's picture daily for one hundred years. My father says we cannot believe anything which comes in *National Herald*.'

Everyone nodded in agreement. David's father was respected among us.

'He's alive, he's alive I tell you.' I yelled to my little brother who was standing like the leg-umpire near Kéya: 'Go and phone Arren Uncle and ask him if Chacha Nehru is alive or dead.'

No politician's life had ever impinged so agonizingly on mine. I needed very little time. On that day a maiden century had the urgency of a whole life's work; to fall short when so close seemed like death. If only I could have got my runs, I would happily have killed every Indian politician myself, Prime Minister downwards.

Or perhaps not quite all. Nehru would have been the exception, and on that afternoon when Kéya's announcement sullied the air, it was the fact that she had spoken of Nehru and no one less which, for all my anxiety to play on, gave me pause. I knew that for our parents Nehru was a holy cow. The timbre of their voices when they spoke of him conveyed nearly as much affection as when they said anything about Mahatma Gandhi. Nehru wasn't God incarnate, but he was St Peter to the great soul whose chin was later chewed up by silverfish as surely as a cow making its way through a piano concerto.

Or was it some dim recollection within us of Nehru's visit to our school which prevented further play?

Nehru had arrived wearing a tight-collar jacket with a rose in the lapel. We sang the national anthem and waved the tricolour for him. On the school lawns there was a hutch in which white furry rabbits with red eyes nibbled green lettuce leaves, devouring what we fed them with the dispatch of a cow chewing the Amen Chorus. In the Prime Minister's honour three girls were put on makeshift spinning wheels to spin khadi, demonstrating the country's commitment to handicraft, and three boys were deputed to show him the school's toy model of a diesel locomotive, suggesting the nation's secular commitment to industry. In the sky above a Soviet Packet aeroplane droned towards a landing stretch then called an aerodrome, its stomach full of army jeeps which would flounder and fail on mountain passes near the Pangong Lake. Three national birds, hastily bought for the occasion, were left to display their plumage and strut among roses in the school lawn. Those peacocks walked with their necks, their beaks darting at petals which had fallen off dismembered roses called Kennedy and Nehru. From the distance of our classroom they looked like thick mobile beds of blue roses straining an unwieldy path through the green.

Nehru was pleased. He loved children, or perhaps pretended he did better than most grown people. He visited the nursery and picked up Kéya with a swoop of affection but she, alarmed, began crying and pissed all over his jacket.

Nehru's unruffled reaction to Kéya may have helped us learn why he was the one Indian politician we wouldn't murder. He hadn't been disgusted, nor had he gruffly handed Kéya over to her teacher. He'd laughed off his wetness, then sat alongside Kéya and her friends and soothed them with a story. At the end of it Kéya was quite dry-eyed and willing enough to give Chacha Nehru a parting kiss.

Perhaps on that day of my ruined century I held inside some

remembrance of that lost time. I said: 'Let's play till we know for sure, if Arren Uncle says he's dead, we'll stop.'

But my brother failed me in the hour of my need. He poked his head clear over the balcony. He said: 'Gupta Aunty is crying. Arren Uncle says Prime Minister has just now dieded.'

Years later when I sat in a class listening to a slightly balding lecturer in a Nehru jacket who said 'for whom the bell tolls isn't Hemingway, it's Donne . . .', I switched off the sermon, I didn't listen any more, I didn't hear the explanation which followed because the provenance of those words was a fragrance from that day I failed to score a century and a prime minister died; or it may have been that there were roses in the lawn outside which gave the lecturer's words the scent of Nehru, who liked children and wrote fine prose and put roses into the buttonholes of his tight-collar jacket; or some stray coalescence of sights and sounds which recalled in me the dull finality with which a small umpire tolled the knell of our cricket game.

My brother's announcement settled the issue. Jawaharlal Nehru, lover of roses in buttonholes, uncle to every Indian kid, was dead. The bails were off, the game was up. I uprooted the wickets, feeling betrayed, fighting back the mist in my eyes.

'Let's go home,' I said to my brother on the balcony.

Mrs Gayatri Gupta waddled to the balcony with tears in her eyes just then. 'What's all the shouting downstairs? Don't you know what has happened?' she asked. Then she saw the disconsolate look on my face. 'Come upstairs please,' she said, 'this is the time when we should be together.'

We shook the dust off the past and trooped up to Mrs Gupta's flat.

Mrs Gupta prayed a lot and made prestations for good health, good looks and Kéya's marriage to a rich man. The prestations took the form of yellow sweets in translucent cups made of thin blotting paper which soaked up the excess grease. The Guptas had a blackish dachshund called Kaloo, who, being universally desired, was pet-named Coca Cola. When Mrs Gupta gave us sweets Coca Cola looked at us with anxious eyes. We ate the sweets slowly, watching the changes of expression on Coca Cola's face. Her anxiety made her lift one paw involuntarily, as if to shake hands, after which she pretended lack of interest while licking her jowls. When that drew no response from us, she gave a little bark. After that ritual bark we gave her the rich blotting paper, which she ate up. Then her eyes took on a satisfied expression.

The blotting paper had the name of the shop inscribed on it in understated, pale pink letters: 'Chowdhury Sweet House', it said, and the box from which the sweets emerged said in bold letters, rather mysteriously:

MILK IS NOT SOLD IN THIS ESTABLISHMENT

as though the first thing people would assume upon entering Chowdhury Sweet House was that milk must be the one thing it undoubtedly sold. In actual fact about the only thing it ever sold was those delicious yellow sweets, which were ranged coldly on shelves among sweets of different colours. You could see them line the whole shop, yards and yards of them, glistening and sticky inside their cups. I never managed to discover why the owners of Chowdhury Sweet House so strenuously proclaimed on their boxes that they did not sell milk.

Coca Cola did not, in any case, like milk, whether from Chowdhury's or elsewhere. She liked bananas. A bicycling fruit-seller pedalled his wares in our neighbourhood most mornings, and we woke to his cries. Kéya would rush out and buy a ripe bunch to feed Coca Cola her breakfast. She peeled bananas with great expertise, and Coca Cola ate them all with equal relish. When she was ten years old and the movements of Beethoven's 'Emperor' Concerto had fallen to the slower clarity of 33 revolutions per minute, my brother gave Kéya a faster record which went at 45 r.p.m. Inside it Harry Belafonte sang 'Come Mr Tally-man, tally me banana.' I imagined Coca Cola's stomach as a yellow cylinder made up of bananas and sweet blotting paper, with 'Chowdhury

Sweet House' advertised in the region of her intestines. My brother never sipped dark-coloured soft-drinks from a bottle because it made him think he was draining out the insides of a dachshund. He always used a glass.

Coca Cola's mistress, Mrs Gupta, Kéya's mother, had been a teacher of Sanskrit at a girls' school until, for some reason which no doctor could diagnose, she developed an itinerant clot in her brain. Amma, who distrusted Mrs Gupta's immersion in Hinduism, said it was the only formulation she was capable of. Some days the clot travelled to a sensitive sector of Mrs Gupta's mind and drove her insane. Then we heard her scream in High Hindi at her husband, who spent much time examining his face in a mirror, showering the dark patches which came to light with snowstorms of Ponds Talcum.

Mr Gupta's widowed sister, Mrs Bhargava, lived with them. She got yelled at too because she burnt one-rupee notes in the prayer room. Each day she burnt some paper money in front of a garlanded picture of Mr Bhargava, her dead husband, as penance for denying him cigarettes while he was alive. She believed the smoke ascended to heaven where he sat cigaretteless, waiting to inhale and forgive his wife. Soon after his death in a road accident on a German highway she had tried to buy some straightforward forgiveness behind her sister-in-law's back by lighting up cigarettes before his picture in the prayer room, but the smell of Wills Filter and some specks of tobacco ash had given her away. When Mrs Gupta realized what was happening inside her own sacristy, the clot in her brain moved with such violence that she was left speechless for days. This might have seemed a good reason for continuing with cigarettes, but even Mr Gupta was sufficiently distracted from his face by his sister's profanity. He protested, his wife's clot was dislodged, her livid silence improved into screams of Sanskrit, and Mrs Bhargava betook herself to the bank for a crisp wad of one-rupee notes. After that her prayers consisted of a short mumble and a long ritual during which she neatly rolled a note into the shape of a cigarette, stuffed it full of holy inflammables, licked it in place like a professional, lit it with her dead husband's favourite Dunhill lighter, and watched in a haze of penitence as the smoke rose towards him.

We knew Mr Bhargava only from his picture, which was in the worship room. Mr Bhargava looked a bit like Clark Gable. He had a thin moustache and wore a pin-stripe suit with a Nehruvian rose on the lapel. He stood within a florid pantheon of gods and goddesses festooned with rivers, snakes, Sanskrit slokas and fleshy arms. Below his picture it said:

SHRI JWALA PRASAD BHARGAVA WHO DEPARTED
FOR HIS HEAVENLY ABODE IN WEST GERMANY
ON 23RD SEPT. 1958.

and in smaller type it said 'Delhi Picture Mart, Parathe Wali Gali, Delhi 1957'. Near his picture there was bright blue Devanagari calligraphy in another frame: 'Gajananum, Bhoot, Gun, Adi Sevitum'. I found out this meant 'Elephants, Devils, Spirits, etc. are at Your Service.' It was an epitaph which confused me, for if it was true that Mr Bhargava was being serviced by the underworld, puffs of smoke were unlikely to be in short supply. Looking at the expression on Mr Bhargava's face I secretly believed that he was in fact smoking himself silly, and I felt bad for Mrs Bhargava who so optimistically assumed that her husband was enthroned in the company of angels.

Kéya Gupta's first-floor house looked over the railway line and beyond to our flat, and on that day in the early sixties when Nehru died, as we reached her balcony, we saw Amma and Mrs Arren cross the tracks and come towards the cricket pitch below.

'Amma amma,' shouted my brother, 'come upstairs. This is time for together. We are going to pray for Nehru Chacha.'

The two women came up the stairs. I turned to communicate my cricketing agony to my mother and saw her in a faded white sari, so different from the flamboyant colours she usually wore, and there were tears in her eyes. Mrs Arren was sobbing into a handkerchief and clinging to my mother. It was bewildering. Amma, who I'd never seen more than curtly sociable with our

16

neighbours, held out her hand to Mrs Gupta, and the three women, our own mothers, wept together.

I felt a mixture of protectiveness and alarm at this strange spectacle. What could my mother, who had always seemed so invulnerable, possibly have felt to break down at the death of a man in the radio, a politician in the air? What could she *really* have felt, I wondered. There was no doubt in my mind that her feelings were real. Amma was blunt and wore her heart on her sleeve, and I knew she could not feign social sympathy. But I had no visual correlative with which to figure out my mother's inner being, nothing with which to imagine her insides in the way my brother and I looked at Coca Cola. I simply forgot my own sorrow at the sight of her tears and realized that Nehru meant something deeper and far more emotional than an unfinished innings.

Soon Kéya's house was full of people. Our fathers were back from their offices and shops, and the holiness of the Gupta household somehow made it the right place in which to congregate for the occasion. Dr Modi, who was a surgeon, diagnosed the cause of Nehru's death in the light of professional experience:

'He died with a Chinese bayonet in his heart,' he said.

'Not even one injection,' said Dr (Mrs) Modi, who was an anaesthetist in her waking hours. 'They only gave him tablets. What can tablets do? If they had given him some injections Panditji would be with us today.'

The Modis were Farookh's parents, and between them they had put to sleep and cut up most of the people in our town. After surgery Dr Modi read P.G. Wodehouse to repair his soul against the butcheries of the day. Later in the evening he made loud sucking noises into a walnut tobacco pipe while working his jugular vein and gazing with eyes popping out at two green parrots squawking against their cage. He was fond of metaphors. When friends or clients came to see Dr Modi, he asked them to perch, perch.

Dr (Mrs) Modi advertised herself as MBBS (Luck.), MD (Mad.). Abba expanded the abbreviations as 'Lucknow' and 'Madras', but

17

Amma said they could equally mean that Dr (Mrs) Modi, though off her head, had fate and fortune unaccountably on her side. Dr (Mrs) Modi was seldom seen. After administering her injections she came home and took one herself. She slept so hard that there were never any bananas in her house. Sleepiness was a trait Farookh inherited from his mother, except on that occasion when he removed the bails from my wickets the afternoon that Nehru died.

'Please come this way into the prayer room,' said Mrs Bhargava, 'so that we may pray for the soul of Panditji.'

'His soul, but . . . well yes, yes, I suppose . . .' said Abba uncertainly, looking with concern at Amma. But he joined in as everyone took off their sandals and proceeded with them towards the memorial service. Even Ramesh and Pramesh, who were poor and therefore diffident about entering our affluent houses, looked at home at Kéya's that evening, with Coca Cola sniffing at the new smell of their legs.

'If I may be permitted,' said Mr Arren to the congregation, clutching a book, 'I should like to read a small passage from Pandit Nehru's *Autobiography*, if no one has any objection.'

Mrs Gupta and Mrs Bhargava looked doubtful and displaced, but Skylab Singh's father generously extended hospitality of the house to Mr Arren.

'Yes yes of course, no objection, what objection shobjection?' he said with surprising kindness, for he subscribed to the *National Herald* and was Mr Arren's bitter enemy: he had even taken to tipping his daily house-rubbish into the Arren garden. This made Mrs Arren furious, but her own voice never rose above a squeak and she failed to incite retaliation in her husband because he was too busy writing newsreports and novels. Mr Arren was our badminton coach and wrote his novels at night on a clattering Remington. The typewriter had been submerged during the flood of 1960 and the arm of the letter 'e', weakened with use and water, had broken off. Mr Arren typed 'c' in its place and filled up all the gaps with a Ladies Shaeffers ink-pen. Most of his time on fiction was spent looking for 'c's to fill up, first on the top copy, then on its carbon. The most difficult sentence he ever wrote was 'For cast is cast and wcst is wcst, and nc'cr thc twain shall mcct.' Each time he finished a novel he kept the lower sheets, stapled the fair ones carefully into chapters, rubberbanded the whole and sent it in a registered airmail packet to 'The Chief Editor, Nobel Prize for Literature, Stockholm, Sweden.' Mr Arren had written seven novels, all held together by rubberbands. 'He will definitely win it,' said my father when I told him Mr Arren had applied for the Nobel Prize, 'unless they feel his work doesn't quite hold together.' For three years after that, when Mr Arren got annually beaten in Stockholm, I attributed his unsuccess to the age of his typewriter and the amazing negligence with which he bound his fiction. But Mr Arren's masterwork did come to light more locally, many years later, when his son David demonstrated a powerful backhand smash which won him the town's Junior Bad-minton Championship. Some time after that, with casual perfidy, Mr Arren joined the *National Herald*, but on that evening he turned his literary interest to good use as a sermon.

'This is from Nehru, Chapter XLVII,' he said, 'the chapter is entitled "What is Religion?" Here Nehruji is talking about what is religion really. Now, with your permission, I will . . .'

At this point Coca Cola, who was not normally allowed into the sanctum, got her tail stepped on by Ramesh and yelped, then snapped at Ramesh's ankles; Ramesh screamed and pushed into Mrs Bhargava, who crashed straight into the arms of her dead husband, overbalanced, and fell over him on the floor, from which position the loving couple were sundered and placed in an upright position by all the ladies. Mrs Bhargava moaned loudly. Ramesh fled the room and stood outside. Kéya was alarmed for Coca Cola, who she picked up and deposited in the corridor. Mr Arren cleared his throat.

'So, here Nehruji is saying . . .'

'Yes yes yes, he is saying about religion, but not one religions but all religion, and Arren sahab in the same book if I am not mistaken he has also said about Guru Nanak and Sikhism and also about Chinese and whichever religion is over there . . .'

'Tao,' said Abba, interrupting Mr Singh.

'Thou? What is thou? That is in Christian religion ji, but I am talking about Chinese religion not about Christian religion, but of course Nehruji also believed in all religion and . . .'

'And in none too,' said Abba hastily.

'Nun? O yes of course, in nuns also he believed and in fact even in monks and brothers also but . . .'

'Exactly exactly,' said Mr Arren, cutting in hastily, 'BUT. That is a good word, BUT, because it shows us that there are at least two sides to everything, what is holy in the holy cow BUT also what is . . .'

'Yes exactly,' said Abba, 'and I think even as we pray for Nehru we should remember that his motto was "Lord I disbelieve, help thou my unbelief." '

'Thou,' muttered Mr Singh, 'what thou? That word I think seems to be your favourite . . .'

'Wait wait, please wait,' said Mr Arren, throwing up his hands, 'this is exactly what I would like to demonstrate by reading this extract. Now please . . . whatever we all have said, that is what Nehru has already said in this: now please, I quote –

I felt lonely and homeless, and India, to whom I had given my love and for whom I had laboured, seemed a strange and bewildering land to me. Was it my fault that I could not enter into the spirit and ways of thinking of my countrymen? Even with my closest associates I felt that an invisible barrier came between us and, unhappy at being unable to overcome it, I shrank back into my shell. The old world seemed to envelop them, the old world of past ideologies, hopes and desires. The new world was yet far distant.

> Wandering between two worlds, one dead,
> The other powerless to be born,
> With nowhere yet to rest his head.

India is supposed to be a religious country above everything else, and Hindus and Moslems and Sikhs and others take pride in their faiths and testify to their truth by breaking heads. The spectacle of what is called religion . . .

'Aachhoo, aachhoo,' said Skylab's mother, making everyone in the prayer-room jump. 'Aachhoo Minduruh, aachhoo Minduruh,' she went again, this time appealing after each sneeze to her husband, who was spelt Mahinder and called Minduruh.

'Arré darling,' said her husband solicitously.

Mrs Singh wiped her nose with her sleeve. 'Flowers, oh these flowers, every time they are giving me allergic sneeze. How was Nehruji wearing rose all day, that I don't know, but now he is no more. I'm so sorry. Please . . .'

Mr Arren cleared his throat.

. . . what is called religion, or at any rate organized religion, in India and elsewhere has filled me with horror . . . And yet I knew well that there was something else in it which supplied a deep inner craving of human beings. How else could it have been the tremendous power it has been and brought peace and comfort to innumerable tortured souls? Was that peace merely the shelter of blind belief and absence of questioning, the calm that comes of being safe in harbour, protected from the storms of the open sea, or was it something more? In some cases certainly it was something more . . . I am afraid it is impossible for me to seek harbourage in this way. I prefer the open sea, with all its storms and tempests. Nor am I greatly interested in the afterlife . . .

At this point Mrs Singh's allergy to pollen developed into an uproar of sneezes which drowned Mr Arren entirely, and when she subsided we heard lamentations intoning spontaneously out of Mrs Gupta. Mrs Singh's sneezing seemed to have moved her clot into its loquacious Sanskrit position and very soon her orisons invoked every god worth the name, in addition to ele-phants, spirits, etc.

Oddly enough, everyone seemed equally touched and moved by the nasal chanting. Dr (Mrs) Modi, Mrs Dewan, and round Mrs Bhargava swelled the chorus. Mr Singh placed the flower vase at a sufficient distance from his wife's nose. A parish congregation of listeners became a crowd of sorrowing, uncertain Hindus whose religious affiliations dissolved within a common mist which covered their eyes in honour of Nehru. The church-going Arrens, the tipsy Dewans, the turbaned Singhs, the Sanskritized Guptas, the knife-wielding sleep-ridden Modis, and even my parents, agnostics like Nehru, showed no impatience in Kéya's family prayer-room. I saw them all listen with bowed heads and after a while the tears returned to Amma's eyes and wouldn't stop streaming down her face. My brother went and sat on her lap during the prayers, and perhaps I looked disturbed, for Abba put his arm round my shoulder as Mrs Gupta's Rigvedic canticle moved towards infinity, accompanied by Mrs Bhargava's mum-bles. In front of them an array of gods and goddesses sat unmoved, and Mr Bhargava with his impish Clark Gable grin awaited the smoke of his daily cigarette.

'Let's get out,' I said to the others as soon as the prayers were over. 'There aren't any sweets today. Let's get to the tracks.'

'No, wait, it's not dark yet, I'll get my kite,' said Mohan.

'Okay,' said Intelligent, 'but after that we'll walk on the track.'

'Yes,' said Skylab, 'but after that . . .'

'. . . we'll walk on the track,' said everyone else.

Mohan rushed off and reappeared with a kite painted the colours of the Indian flag. It was a dull, breezeless day, but Mohan managed to get it going. It rose in the air, hovered over a skein of electric lines, spinning and fluttering feebly. Mohan was the only one who could have kept it going, but in the west the orange sky of evening was dying away and the rest of us wanted to explore the country further afield. David snatched the string off Mohan and ran down the track with it. Mohan chased him furiously, so Farookh took over the kite-string, with the result that the kite struck a telegraph pole and swooped down onto the track. It was dragged a short distance and collapsed with a gash through its midriff.

'Just look what yoll've done men,' screamed Mohan.

'Aw come on yoll men,' screamed back Intelligent. 'We'll get another kite tomorrow. Yoll want to walk or no?'

'Yoll want to walk or no?' screamed his satellite.

Mohan was persuaded against grief and we began the final ritual of our evenings, a soothing march into the landscape which stretched before us like a needle endlessly pointed. After the course of an entire day, when the spaces of our minds were congested with flurries of traffic and tumult of feelings, the straightforward emptiness of the railway track worked on our bodies like the tranquillizing palliative of an enormous lake and harboured us against the turbulence of the open sea.

If you looked sharp left down one side of the tracks, you could see the huge banyan tree by the road where Ramesh and Pramesh lived with their father, Parmeshwar, in a wayside shack. As we hopped along the wooden sleepers we saw him emerge from his hut, walk a short distance, hitch up his pyjamas and water the track. His entire family's excretory functions depended on the railways, for only the sight and sound of passing trains automatically caused in them the necessary muscular relaxation. On Sundays, when there was no morning train on the broad-gauge track of their home, the boys looked constipated but their father made his way on a bicycle held together by rope, balancing a can of water in one hand, towards the sound of the Naini Tal Express on the metre gauge.

Pissing was one of the two things with which Ramesh was dexterous. Both he and his twin were equally adept at spraying nails on the road: on some days, when their puncture-repair business was bad, they depended on it for their livelihood. They sat under a tree with a wooden toolbox about a kilometre ahead of the sprayed nails, while Parmeshwar sat with a duplicate wooden toolbox about the same distance from the nails in the opposite direction. When car, scooter and cycle drivers drove up with wobbling tyres, they looked at them with indifferent sympathy and got to work. For these emergency days Parmeshwar always bought the sharpest nails from the most reputed ironmonger in town, and the nails proved a godsend, yielding him and his two sons enough holes to make a subsistence wage. During the day Pramesh and Ramesh were busy heating bits of rubber and sticking them as patches on torn tubes. In the evenings they played cricket with us, for towards sunset their father Parmeshwar took over the business and ran it along other ingenious lines.

He paid a small monthly commission on sales to Habib, the railway gate-man, in return for which Habib developed his physique all day long by winching two gigantic iron lines of latitude down from the sky. These served to block the traffic from the track, which ran equatorially through the middle of the gate. It was Habib's job to create the tropics and cause traffic jams on either side of the road for as long as humanly possible. Cycle and scooter riders managed to wheel their vehicles through the doldrums by ducking their heads or squeezing through the heavenly descent of geography, but the cars, less manoeuvrable, waited against the barriers for the train to pass, like water at a sluice gate. Meanwhile Parmeshwar busied himself among the car drivers and their passengers, selling them peanuts in winter and white radishes or cucumbers in summer. He and his sons ate all the leftovers for dinner. Ramesh and Pramesh looked nut-brown in summer and watery-pale in the winter. On Tuesdays, the weekly holy day, Parmeshwar took a short-term lease on a cow from the neighbourhood milkman and caparisoned her for the evening in the trappings and suits of religion. The cow looked nothing like Mrs Gupta. She looked like a medieval warhorse decked up for a joust, only awaiting Ivanhoe or Sir Lancelot to jump on and take off. Parmeshwar, less Arthurian, had more dignified ends in view. He paraded her in the vicinity of a makeshift temple, which he set up by the blocked road with a few stolen bricks, and collected alms from the traffic well into the night, helped by his two sons.

Despite his poverty, Parmeshwar never seemed ill-tempered or wanting in contentment. He stubbed his beedi against a fishplate and hailed us: 'It's time for the Agra Mail, better watch out.'

'Will it come today?' I asked. 'Have you heard that Nehruji is dead?'

Parmeshwar settled himself on his haunches and spat into the air. He fished for his wad of tobacco and began grinding it on the palm of his hand. For a while he gazed at it, moving the muscles of his palm to adjust the matter into a satisfactory position, then with a swift upward jerk he gulped the granules. After that he groped for his beedis and, three matches later, puffed at a tiny glow. 'So what did you say? Nehruji is dead? Are you sure?'

'Today,' said Farookh, 'little while back.'

The glow in Parmeshwar's lips had dimmed. He puffed vigorously and fiddled afresh in his pockets. 'Any of you boys got some matches? Naah. These are bad days. Did he die in Agra?'

'He died in capital,' said Intelligent. 'Agra is for mad people.'

'Well,' said Parmeshwar, 'Agra Mail will come. Definitely. It will come late and prices will rise early. Gandhiji died in Delhi also but Agra Mail still came, only four hours late.'

He moved the muscles of his mouth to accumulate phlegm and spat at the track.

'After that prices went up. Now Nehruji is dead and the same thing will happen. These days all trains are running late and rubber is costly. British days have gone. Nehruji made them go. Now we have got freedom and quick rubber solutions in toothpaste tubes.' He bent to put his hand on the track, feeling its pulse. 'But still the trains are running late. The signal is up but soon it will be down.'

The wires which ran along the track rattled and shook. A signal post, standing on one leg like a solitary stork, lowered its beak.

The silhouette of its single eye changed from rabbit red to peacock green.

Parmeshwar paused. 'There, I can sense it coming. You boys can walk on, but better watch out.'

A slow steam engine which looked like a gigantic dachshund came up billowing smoke, puffing and heaving. It passed by Habib's railway bars which lay prone between Kéya's house and ours. As the train passed we saw the bars reluctantly rise in an arc which pointed them up like slim uncertain rockets aimed at a sky in which dachshunds and Soviet cosmonauts strapped in space, descended of Yuri Gagarin and Laika, the hound of heaven, encircled the globe. Below, the impatient traffic escaped pellmell over the tracks and disappeared into the horizon.

Now the sun was down: paint could not hope to reproduce the faint half flush which died along the sky. We tracked our way back, skipping sleepers, passing cowherds who drove their animals home. The dust rose in the air and covered the animals which moved through the sunset. In my mind the haze congealed the cows into an image of Mrs Gupta, and as we walked the railway track branched out into many lines, many lives. Ramesh and Pramesh dropped off at their shack by the banyan tree, the rest of us at other points along the glistening equatorial gridirons, beckoned by lights which flickered through the windows of our separate homes.

Inside, All India Radio crackled out material for a new dictionary of clichés deep into the night. An epoch had ended, a tearful nation mourned the departed soul, the light had gone out of our lives, a new era would have to dawn. A fertile stream of rhetorical bilge, which neither Nehru's prose nor his reign had managed to undermine, emerged through static. 'In accordance with his wishes, Pandit Nehru's ashes will be scattered over the many different regions of India, over the Himalayas, and over the water of the Ganga, over the hills and the plains of his beloved Bharat . . .'

The stream of words about Nehru flowed on and on, world

without end, like the slokas in Kéya Gupta's house, and all the while Nehru's ash fell as an aura over army jeeps which jutted like jagged teeth through white snows upon the navy-blue of the Pangong Lake, over necks which dragged blue flowerbeds behind them, over cows and the erasures of silverfish undeterred by the halo of martyrs. The shadow of Nehru hung like a mist over the universe. It had the omniscience of a cow. By the time that day had ended, every image of the world mirrored an epoch and became layered over with the ashen pallor of a mist which carried the remains of Nehru.

That day, that year, stuck like an anchor to the sea-floor of our drifting minds. We moved to our second home, a bungalow which overlooked flowering trees, in the winter of the year that Nehru died.

2

Murder in May

In the late summer of that year we lived in a house on a road that looked across flowering branches of gulmohar and amaltas to a tailor's shop. The orange of the gulmohar and the yellow of the amaltas seemed like brave flourishes of dissent against the heat of that depraved May which devastated our town with such gratuitous ferocity. February had beguiled us with cool breezes and sometimes showers, March with the deception of winter's last fling, and then overnight April turned with a burst of flowers into May. So vengeful was the sun and so vivid the colours which flamed in protest against its gigantic horror that it was impossible not to remember the names of those trees. For five searing weeks when the rest of the world fled towards water and the snow of the mountains, the gulmohar and the amaltas stood their ground like General Custer, sprouting fire against the intransigent sky.

It was some relief to look at the silent colour of defiance on those trees. All day they stood sentinel outside our house, dripping bloom. Inside, we dripped sweat. The electricity, like the servants, would come and go without warning. The water was much more predictable: it didn't bother to come at all. If you switched open the tap in the day you could hear inside it the death rattle of a very old man. By late evening he seemed to have recuperated enough for a sluggish trickle to gargle and sputter out in the bathroom, as slow as a government clerk. It took even more time to fill a bucket than it did to get one's savings out of the State Bank.

There was nothing to do but sweat it out. In between virtually waterless baths I read *Treasure Island* and heard Beethoven's music in which at times I caught the sublime heroism of emperors, or the birdsong happiness of pastoral worlds, or my body afloat at the extremities of the Milky Way.

Reality was rather different. My little brother and I were awoken each day by the silence of slowing fans as the electricity went and the flies came. The earliest sensation in our happy home was the tickle of flies making their breakfast off our body salts. The earliest sounds in our happy home were curses.

'O god, not again,' was Amma's opener. Being female, she had no option but restraint.

'Those bastards, those bloody bastards, those bloody swines, they should all be electrocuted,' was how Abba began the day. His wrath at the electricity department took many cups of tea and several newspapers to simmer down into a general feeling of disgust with India as a whole.

'This damn country, I tell you, it's going to the dogs.' He achieved a little catharsis by the globalization of personal discomfort.

'No it isn't,' said Amma. 'It's already gone to the flies. Now move your backside and do something about it.' She had a low wrath threshold.

Abba grouched. Within the house he was the helpless Indian male. The kitchen was out of bounds for him ever since he tried to light the kerosene stove and nearly burnt the house down, and it was as much as he could do to put the newspapers to good use. Yawning and groaning, he folded one to a handy size and worked it as an impromptu Japanese fan against the absence of electricity and the ubiquity of the flies. Then, since his mind and bowels were controlled by the print media, he hitched up his pyjamas and began his jet propulsion towards the loo, all the while muttering against the foulness of the weather, the stupidity of the Indian government, the animus of servants, and the malign conspiracies of fate which all seemed personally directed at him. Clutching the papers, he thrashed at flies and yelled for the ayah to give him more tea. '*Something* was rotten in the state of Denmark. *Everything* is rotten with the state of bloody India.' Such sentiments from him marked our transition to full-blooded summer.

Each morning Abba emerged from the toilet to make his matutinal pronouncement about the previous day's temperature, as though he had something personal to do with its inexorable increase.

'One hundred and seven in the shade,' he said with satisfaction one morning, after we had fanned our way in Hawaii chappals to the breakfast table. He preferred the Fahrenheit scale to the Centigrade because the numbers on it sounded more impressive.

'Fifteen dead by heatstroke in Bara Banki in one day. And on the other side sixty-three have drowned in the Assam floods. Twenty-eight feared washed away in Hooghly ferry capsize. Bus plunges into khud near Simla. Drought conditions take toll in tribal belt. Small pox claims eight victims in Bihar. All in one day! What is happening to this country, I tell you?'

He seemed perversely pleased, nonetheless, that it had all happened in one day; if it had happened over two the newspapers would have been less stimulating. In some obscure way his sense of self increased after he had registered the rise in temperature and chewed awhile on the statistics in the papers. The higher the temperature, the more the deaths reported, the greater seemed his sense of self-achievement in having fought off the deliberate cruelties being directed against him by the Union of India.

That morning his attention was diverted by the flies on his bowl of mangoes. Cautiously, like a leopard in sight of prey, he quadrupled the newspaper, then swatted hard with a little Tarzan yelp. Two flies flattened into red-black gore on newsprint and were examined by the killer, his catharsis now reinforced by a small sense of triumph against the country and the heat.

'This is India,' he said, disgust mingling with satisfaction. 'All unity in diversity. So many deaths in one day.'

I picked up the paper and examined it with morbid delight.

'Fifteen men on a dead man's chest, Yo ho ho and a bottle of rum.'

Amma wasn't amused by this casual heartlessness. 'That's not very nice,' she said sharply. 'Those are poor people. How would you feel if you had to live out on the road or were washed away in a flood?'

Very dry and very wet, I thought, but held my tongue and searched within for a less obviously rude retort. 'How Would You Feel If' was the standard moral line with which all parents began . . . they only had to fill in the blanks with something or other to make you feel guilty.

'Then why are you eating mangoes?' I asked defiantly.

Abba warded off the darkening of Amma's brows against me with casual expertise. 'That,' he said to me with a guarded glance in her direction, 'is a non sequitur. And for your information, and also for the information of your dear Amma, a non sequitur is something that has no logical connection with what has gone before.'

I lay low and said nothing. I had discovered that silence usually helped restore things to an equable temperature. Amma was about to come out with some scathing answer but fortunately my little brother diverted them both with his own non sequitur.

'Amma Amma, my teacher aunty told me to say Papa-Mummie. She told me to say Papa-Mummie, not to say Abba-Amma. Yesterday she told me you are my Mummie and she says to call Abba Papa like all my friends.'

My brother only said anything if he was feeling overwhelmed enough for the words to spill out of him, so everyone listened when he spoke as though they'd heard the first cuckoo of spring. His interruption lowered the Fahrenheit and switched my parents on to a tricky elementary problem. The everyday difficulties of secularism compounded the heat, the dust, the drought, the floods, the government, the electricity, the water. 'In India,' said Abba, 'the rich are too rich to care and the poor are too poor to care. It's only people like us who have to suffer.' It was only in

India that the entire universe had come together to conspire against the middle class. Even in that small house where we lived in the late summer of that year, given breath by the gulmohar and the amaltas and by ceiling fans which blew the tepid air towards the hotter air outside, there seemed such a basic quality about the problems of managing to stay alive.

'I will speak to your teacher,' said Amma. 'Don't worry. Some children like to call their parents Mummie-Papa, other children like to call them Amma-Abba. In our house we like Amma-Abba.'

My father and she exchanged looks. My little brother looked uncertain, but he forgot his worries at the sight of mangoes. He liked Dasehris, I liked Langdas, Amma liked Chausas, and Abba ate every variety of them faster than we liked. Soon we were all making loud sucking noises with our mangoes, looking furtively left and right to estimate how many we might be able to wolf before the others did.

Somewhere outside, fifteen men had shrivelled into the earth for lack of water. A little further, many more had been carried away by an excess of it. In my book that summer they linked up with the water in the sea over which pirates carried a dead man's chest, and in all our lives they linked up with the sweet and salt juices of summer that went in or came out of our bodies. Everything was connected or seemed connectable with everything else: drought with flood, mangoes with sweat, death with rum, newspapers with bowels, Amma-Abba with Mummie-Papa, Bara Banki with Assam. The unity-within-diversity of our landscape seemed just a question of who made the connections, and I didn't see how the pirates in *Treasure Island* were a non sequitur to the newspaper deaths if the mangoes descending into our stomachs weren't. Anyway, the stray constructions which comprised the country in my mind seemed incomparably more delightful than the gloomy pictures of it that Abba provided from his wad of papers. The newspaper reports only seemed like bad fiction. They contained no stories that moved me to sympathy or to feeling of any kind, only damp or dry clichés which I felt vaguely obliged to take seriously out of filial guilt. Inside myself I was dubious about people who read newspapers like the gospel.

In the tailor's shop two sewing machines, their brand names faded smooth by use, whirred busily all day. Their circular sounds mingled with the rotating rattle of a table fan which blew hot air at Masterji, as he was called, and his brother the dwarf. The dwarf, as befitting his size, had even less name, and was called Chhoté, or Kaddu, or Bauné, or Thigné, all words that connoted someone lacking in stature. To my mind those names were all unfair to the little tailor, who always welcomed the neighbourhood children to his shop and enthralled us with the intricacies of his sewing machine. Most of his life he sat huddled self-effacingly in one corner with his little legs crossed over, peering at cloth and thread, studiously cranking his machine, always keeping a quiet distance from the taller world of condescending people. He was completely reclusive and never stirred out of his shop. He did not participate in the life of the street, though I'd often seen him stand at the door of his shop to feed stray dogs and give chapatis to the bear man who hung around our road with his bear in tow. But for the most part he kept to himself and thought his own thoughts, and my instinctive sympathies were with him and against the larger world which did not comprehend people below a certain height. I re-read *Snow White* to see if dwarfs could be called something more definite than Chhoté and Bauné but got no help there. I wanted him to have a fuller name, a real name in place of those caricatures. Once I asked Amma what his real name was, but she treated me like a non sequitur.

'Real name? People like that don't really have real names like we have. Anyway, I don't know his real name,' she said, peering at the tail end of a thread. 'How does it matter what his real name is anyway? I don't think he's called anything very much. Your Abba calls him Notre Dame,' she said, biting the thread and manoeuvring it towards an unnecessarily small hole. 'Blast,' she said, glaring at the thread, 'this thing is the size of a camel.'

The camel was having difficulty getting through the eye and I was on the wrong side of the thread of her thoughts.

'Your Abba calls him Notre Dame and I call him Nostradamus,' she said abstractly.

'But why?' I asked, perplexed. 'Are those names his real names?'

She pursed her lips at the camel, pushing him now with studied firmness and letting a stray area of her mind focus on my less important need.

'Those names are real names but they're not his real names,' she said. 'He's a hunchback and some people say he can tell the future. Now go away.'

Grown people were mostly doing something inconsequential. Their lives were lived at some different height and their mysterious explanations were remote from the urgency of my needs. At any rate, I had no desire to compete with a camel for her attention and went off the topic, uncertainly armed with the knowledge that dwarfs reputed to foretell the future could for some reason be called Notre Dame or Nostradamus. I asked Ramu-ki-Amma, our ayah, if she knew his real name, though without much expectation of help. She was a village woman and the concept of a real name was incomprehensible to her. Besides, like everyone her size, she said he was too short to be called anything. I gave up and Hindified my friend the dwarf down to Nasterji, which chimed with his older brother.

I discovered, soon, that the name had taken root. People found it convenient to refer to the pair as Masterji and Nasterji. There was a childish jingle in the combination which pleased everyone and somehow seemed to fit the pair. And with time, as happens when enough people are content to repeat the same phrase or rumour, it took on the apparel of truth. Masterji and Nasterji was what the tailors were called after that, so much so that they themselves accepted the nomenclature without demur. When their shop grew big enough to boast a board it read:

MASTERJI & NASTERJI BROS
LADIS & GENTS TAILORING
VISIT FOR ALL KIND
PANT SHIRT SUITING
PETTY COAT SAREE BLOUSE
GOD MADE MAN
BUT TAILOR MADE GENTAL MAN

The road on which we lived, one house beyond Masterji and Nasterji, had also been named at some distant time in history after a colonial long gone, about whom no one in our town ever knew anything. It was Jackson Road, rechristened Jai Kishan Road to suit the tongues of the people who lived there. Later, to pave the way for its conversion into a middle-class slum, it was renamed Lajwanti Hingorani Chattopadhyaya Marg after the mother of a local nationalist politician whom no one had ever seen.

The pleasant uncertainty of all those names and the absence of history about the place suited the casual amnesia, the lassitude, the restful lack of direction in our town. It was very early in the sixties, the sun was unceasing, and Jai Kishan Road led nowhere in particular. Unnamed cart-tracks and dirt roads fed aimlessly into it, then meandered out at some point in futile, enfeebled efforts to leave the heat behind. Children of dust colour played in the shade of the trees, among idle piles of rocks and mounds of sand and bricks unclaimed for ages. The little boys were always naked waist-down, the little girls always protected strategically by rags. Near them the trees asked no money for their shade to a cobbler, a cigarette-seller, and the street's regular bear man who scratched out a living by flailing his slothful animal into a reluctant dance.

In the evenings a busy little bazaar of vegetables sprouted on the kerb. Men in dhotis and women in old, faded sarees squatted on their haunches or sat stooped by their vegetables, sprinkling the greens and the tomatoes now and then with dashes of water through a net of fingers. Housewives with plastic baskets and husbands riding bicycles on their way home from offices, with cane baskets hooked to their handlebars, stopped and haggled their way towards bargains which satisfied all parties into a grumbling equanimity. From behind the babble of negotiations the children of the thrifty rich emerged out of drawn blinds from bungalows, attracted by the *guddu-guddu-guddu-guddu* sound of the strung pellets with which the bear man's hourglass hand-drum beat out a Pavlovian rhythm to the bear. Everyone awaited the wilting of the amaltas, signalling the sun's cruel victory, which annually enabled the heavens to pelt down the mercy of the monsoon.

I too was part of that world once, watchful and waiting.

On the afternoon of that late May, after the morning ritual of failed electricity, mango juice and the splattered gore of fly on newspaper, before the sun had dulled to the sullen red of evening, I drew a curtain and blinked my way through the colour of the trees towards the inhabitants of the road. I wanted to get out and play the evening's round of cricket and Seven Tiles and Catch-Um-Catch with all the Gooddoos and Pappoos and Babloos and Bantoos of the neighbourhood. But it was not time yet. The tar had melted at the edges of the road and it lay deserted, save for patches of protection from the trees. No one had dared stir out at that hour of the afternoon. The cobbler, the cigarette seller, the ice-cream men and the water sellers with their leaking trolleys had all sought out the shade in some less furious part of town. Only the bear man and his bear were visible.

I saw the bear man slumped next to the bear, close by the cobbler's roof of plastic which served as a ragged gesture of pro-tection. The bear man seemed in a strangely supine position. The bear, however, was unusually active, standing straight up and sniffing the air, looking anxiously to his left and right. Their pos-tures seemed oddly reversed. It was more normal for the bear to be in a slump, or scratching himself with indolent commitment, and for the bear man to be active and coaxing.

I had scarcely noticed this when I saw something even odder.

The door of the tailor's shop burst open and Nasterji rushed out. His expression was intense and his short little body seemed agitated as he blinked and capped his eyes with his hand. It was the first time I had ever seen him fully outside his shop. He looked first to his right and saw nothing, then towards his left, down the road past our house to the bear man and the bear. His expression changed when he saw them and he seemed to look around the road for support. But there was no one on the road. He came to a quick decision and waddled as fast as he could in the direction of the bear, who was still up on his legs, his master still slumped on the kerb. I saw for the first time how small Nasterji really was. There was an anxious sense of purpose in his walk which I did not associate with him.

At Nasterji's approach the bear let out a growl which stopped the little tailor in his tracks. The bear man did not stir, and the bear now bent protectively close to his master, snarling a little to keep the tailor at bay. Nasterji stood at a safe distance, calling out to the bear man.

'Bhaloo Walé,' he said, and then as loud as he could, 'Arré O Bhaloo Walé.' The attractive diffidence of his indoor voice had been overtaken by an urgent, outdoor authority.

But the bear man did not stir. Nasterji edged to his left and right to get a view of the bear man's face. The bear snarled more fiercely and clawed the air as warning, but he was tied and could not venture more than a step or two beyond his master.

Nasterji crouched and waited, calling to the bear man. There was no response. Nasterji bent and I saw him pick a little pebble which he then rolled gently at the bear man. The bear growled and pawed the air, but the bear man lay absolutely still, his face touching the road.

It was then that I recognized what I think Nasterji had sensed sitting inside his shop, and which had seemed urgent enough for him to have made his first appearance on the road. The bear man of Jai Kishan Road had died of the heat. The sun's conquests, so

37

aridly reported in the morning newspapers, had come ironically alive for me.

I stood frozen at my window as Nasterji ran as fast as he could through blasts of heat towards his shop. A moment later he reappeared with Masterji and they both walked hurriedly towards the dead man and the bear. I ran into the recesses of our home to inform Amma and summon her to the window. By the time she arrived, a small crowd of people had begun to gather on the street in a cautious semi-circle some distance from the bear.

The bear now sat beside the body, growling in low tones, uncertain at the changed circumstances in which the crowd had gathered to watch him. The hand-drum to which he responded lay near the body. The bear was now on his own, facing a world of hostile voyeurs, directed only by some inner rhythm which made him protect the body on the kerb.

The crowd swelled as the news spread. People emerged from their homes earlier than they would normally have. Passersby stopped off their bicycles to look, mingling with the louts and dusty urchins who were in the forefront of the semi-circle. Within a few minutes sixty people had emerged out of nowhere, like flies on mangoes, to feed idly upon the dead man and the bear. Life was so routine, the heat so intense, and the sources of entertainment so meagre that even the most minor accident seemed like water to the thirsty gaze of the crowds that formed so miraculously on all our roads. The sudden gathering below was of circus proportions, and that poor man's death was now a major spectacle.

At first the main object of the crowds seemed to be just to look from a safe distance. But then, very quickly, they adjusted to the fact that the bear couldn't get to them, nor they to the body of the bear man. This was satisfactory. It allowed them to move a bit closer. No longer apprehensive or cautious, their morbid curiosity inched them slowly forward.

'Let's make the bear dance,' said one of the louts and picked up a stone. He might have flung it at the animal's feet but Nasterji let out a scream at him. The crowd looked at the dwarf and sniggered.

'Shut up Kaddu,' said the lout. 'Are you in love with the bear?' The crowd laughed.

'Don't you know,' said another, 'dwarfs and bears are all circumcised. Why don't we make them both dance? Don't they look alike?' The crowd roared and scratched itself, preparing for fun.

Masterji shrank back at that but Nasterji stood his ground. Some people in the crowd cackled raucously, others looked uneasy. Two or three old women in the crowd quietly walked away. 'Let's go mun,' said an Anglo-Indian lady in a Doris Day frock to her schoolteacher husband. 'This mob's full of bledgy chhokras and goonda-boys mun.'

'Do not harm the bear,' said Nasterji to the crowd. 'If the bear is harmed, we will drown. Give him some water to drink. Don't you understand? We could all drown.'

The leaders in the crowd swaggered with laughter at the dwarf's comic incoherence. Such a huge agitation in such a diminutive figure had all the disproportion of clowns in the Gemini Circus. It was fun. It provided good entertainment free of cost. What more could one ask for on a summer afternoon?

'Listen to that mad dwarf,' said a man in black drainpipes who had Brylcreem hair slicked back into an Elvis Presley puff. 'He'll drown us if we touch his bear!'

'Call the lunatic asylum,' said another. 'Tell them to lock up the bear and the dwarf.'

'No no yaar, call the zoo,' said a third, his little finger entwined villainously around his neighbour's, 'and tell them to send a cage for the dwarf and the bear.'

There was more laughter. The crowd had now swelled into a swarm of bodies, a hive which thickened by the minute as more and more people ran up so as not to miss out on all the free fun.

I looked helplessly up at Amma.

'I better phone your Abba,' she said, 'and tell him to call the police.' She rustled off in her starched cotton towards the phone.

Amazingly for such a shy man facing so much contempt, Nasterji repeated what he had said. He held his little hands up in the air.

'Wait,' he said with anguish and the little dignity his height allowed, 'please wait. I will get the bear some water. If the bear is harmed we may all be destroyed.'

The man with the Presley puff came into the middle of the circle and began to perform a mocking dance, imitating the bear.

'Don't harm me, don't harm me,' he sang, 'or else I will eat you all . . .'

> O O O, ho ho ho,
> · This bear, this bear, this bear –
> This bear he's got no name, O
>
> Ho ho ho, O O O,
> And me, and me, and me –
> And me I've got no dame, O
>
> Ho ho ho, ho ho ho,
> Bear with me, bear with me, O bear with me –
> O bear will you be my dame, O?

The crowd applauded with gusto. It was now thrilled. The dead man was clearly inaccessible and could be forgotten for the moment. The bear's snarl, watchable earlier, was now monotonous. Dwarfs didn't really have names and animals didn't really have feelings. Those concepts were alien in a world attuned to newspapers in which human beings died like flies in the heat or got washed away as numbers in a flood, noted only for a day in the margins of print. The dwarf possessed neither physical height nor social weight. He had neither significance nor authority. He was probably circumcised. He was comically incoherent. How could he be anything except a figure of fun? Meanwhile, here was Elvis Presley singing in Brylcreem and drainpipes.

'Better get lost quick,' said a grey-haired man to Nasterji, 'or these goondas will feed you to the bear.'

Nasterji stepped back and went off in the direction of his shop.

'Come back Kaddu,' people yelled after him. 'Come and dance for us.'

I heard Amma say something into the phone in the distance.

Elvis had finished his dance and the crowd now awaited something new to happen. The sun was lower on the horizon and the water and ice-cream trolleys had converged to do business on the road. People on the fringes of the crowd dissipated to buy cholera fluid advertised as water for five naya paisa. The better-off bought themselves congealed water sticks advertised as ice-cream – cholera guaranteed or your money back – for four annas a stick. They were replaced by others from the rear who insinuated themselves into hairline spaces within the crush of bodies. They craned their necks to see the dead man and the bear.

A little time passed, a few in the crowd felt entertained enough to depart, others came in to look and hung about to pass the time. The spectacle was slowly losing its entertainment value. The bear man was dead and the bear wasn't performing. The dwarf had departed, the louts had lost some of their pre-eminence. The sun had lowered its relentless gaze and helped to relax the ardour of the crowd. The atmosphere was now less aggressive, less surcharged with expectations of entertainment. With the same unaccountable suddenness with which people had converged, feet began to shift in various directions, leaving only a hard core of idle voyeurs.

But then, just as quickly as the loss of momentum, things livened up again. To everyone's amazement the dwarf came running back, bearing a pitcher of water in one hand and an enamel bowl in the other.

'Welcome, welcome,' said Elvis Presley with a shout which attracted the local Vietnam deserters back to the warfront. Turning to the crowd he anounced in a loud voice, 'And now we shall see a bear drink water and eat a dwarf.'

Nasterji broke through the circle and approached the bear, who growled his warning. The tailor proceeded cautiously, pushing the bowl of water as far forward as he dared, close enough for the bear to drink. Then he retreated and stood near the crowd, watching anxiously to see if the animal would drink. The bear looked at the water but made no move towards it.

'He's not thirsty you fool,' said the grey-haired man. 'Leave him alone and get lost.'

But Nasterji said nothing and just waited.

How long this would have gone on I don't know, but, in keeping with the plot of every Hindi movie, the police arrived on the scene just then to clean things up and end the crowd's fun. I guessed Amma's message had been transmitted on by Abba to his brother, a bureaucrat, who would then have asked some subordinate in the police, in the language of his office, to 'please kindly rush a law-and-order Jeep immediately to the troublespot.'

A grey Mahindra Jeep arrived, trailing clouds of gory black diesel smoke. Five fat policemen stepped out, chewing paan and oozing the greasy authority of people genetically endowed with corruption and brutality. The chief among them was immediately distinguishable by his girth. His paunch was the largest. It overhung a brown gun-belt.

'Hato Hato,' he said belligerently, making it clear that he was now in charge. The crowd took a token step back, waiting to see what would happen next. Only Nasterji, who was now standing, stayed where he was.

'Hey you,' said the chief policeman. His four minions stood just behind, awaiting an order to jump at the dwarf. 'Didn't you hear me you bloody half-witted clown? Get out of the way. We will handle this matter.'

Nasterji walked quickly forward to the enamel bowl and pushed it further towards the bear, then retreated. He knew it was futile to do any more. The bear was confused and alarmed. He snarled to himself and had no mind to drink.

'Don't harm that bear,' said Nasterji to the police. 'If you harm the bear we may drown.'

The crowd laughed. The policeman looked at them in surprise, then joined them with a sneering laugh. He saw that this was no law-and-order situation. This was a circus. He could wait and join the fun. His laughter enlisted the crowd's support in his favour and went against the dwarf. The policeman looked around to check that there was nothing else afoot, no other cause for worry. This crowd wasn't communal. If it erupted at all, it would only be in laughter. There was no real trouble, only a crowd wanting some harmless fun. Some idiot of a bear man had died, leaving his bear tied next to him. Some idiot of a dwarf was being comically protective. He could handle it. But first they would have some fun.

'Get some rope,' he said to his subordinates, who seemed to have a supply of it in their Jeep. 'Now,' he said to the crowd, 'does anyone among you want to lasso the bear?'

An excited murmur went through the crowd and Elvis Presley volunteered at once. A lasso was made and he walked up cautiously, watched by his excited supporters. He threw the noose at the bear, who rose and came savagely forward. Presley turned tail and lunged back into the crowd, and there was a huge surge backwards. People stepped on other people, there were yells, screams, curses. But the bear was held secure by a strong rope and posed no real danger. Soon the crowd pressed forward again and Presley returned to the arena, eager to refurbish his macho image. He tried his hand once more, and then several other times, getting close once, but the rope missed its mark each time.

'Here's someone with a net,' said the grey-haired man to the police chief. 'He's brought a badminton net! Here inspector sahib, catch your bear with the badminton net.'

Fresh excitement. Could the bear be caught in a badminton net? This time the police chief decided to try himself and flung the net with a great gush. But his fingers got caught at one end as

43

he flailed it towards the bear and its rear half landed on his own head.

The crowd roared with laughter. Here was better entertainment than anyone could possibly have bargained for.

'This is our great Indian police!' yelled someone from the back. 'Come and watch our efficient Indian police catch a bear with a badminton net!'

There were bales of hysterical laughter.

'The zoo is going to get three new animals,' shouted another. 'A bear, a dwarf and a policeman!'

Wild laughter and whoops of joy! There were now three hundred people clamouring for a view of the spectacle on Jai Kishan Road.

The policeman, red in the face, looked a circus comedian as he tried to disentangle himself from the net with the assistance of a host of subordinate clowns who had rushed into the mêlée. In their comic collective anxiety they only got in his way, and to the crowd's extreme delight they tripped the fat policeman and he fell flat on his face.

The crowd's joy was now hysterical. It was like watching a Laurel and Hardy film. Even Amma grinned sardonically and I was squealing with laughter. Here was live confirmation of the ineptitude of our police. Here was living demonstration of retribution against the corrupt. Here was comic proof of how the mighty fell!

By the time the policeman extricated himself from the net the crowd was rolling around with laughter and the policeman was purple with rage.

'Move back you bastards,' he yelled hoarsely. 'Move back. I'll show that mother-fucking bear who's in charge here. And as for you lot, shut up or I'll arrest every one of you, you fucking bastards.'

There were residual sniggers, then the crowd fell silent. The policeman looked belligerently in all directions to regain the stature he had lost, and to ensure there was nothing between him and the bear. Then he took the heavy revolver out of his gun-belt. Now the crowd instantaneously transformed itself into an eager whisper of anticipation.

The bear was still near his master, bound by a distance of fifteen feet from the policeman, innocent in his tired, instinctive snarling. The policeman took his time; he had all the time in the world. He pointed his gun in the direction of the bear, slowly and fastidiously, brutally aware of the necessity to stamp his authority forever in the eyes of the crowd.

The policeman took careful aim and fired thrice at the bear's head.

Like John F. Kennedy in the distance to our west, like Vietnamese peasants in the distance to our east, like the flies which sat on our mangoes that morning, that bear never knew what hit him. He slumped down dead in a shaggy black heap over the body of his master. I saw the little dots of red blood that trickled out to mingle with the bear's black hair. The dots spread into a smudge, and I saw the colour of that smudge. It had the tonal discoloration of finality, the hideous emphasis of something which had irrevocably been said. It was a native Indian dye, peculiar to our landscape, yielded by mixing casual brutality with the authority of uniforms and statistics. It was the colour of red-black gore on newsprint, a stain which spread out as one of the indelible colours of the country in my mind.

I cannot exactly recollect if the massive dust-storm which uprooted so many of the gulmohar and amaltas trees on our road in the late summer of that year struck our town on the very same evening that bear was killed, or whether it struck some days later. I don't suppose it matters. Does it even matter that a man I knew slumped with the heatstroke on a barren road and that a bear was shot dead? Does it mean anything at all that a dwarf who had no stature in anyone's eyes gained some in mine? Or that a policeman who lost status entangling himself in a misdirected web emerged a hero by using a gun with such easy precision? You could see all these things connect up with each other. Or you could see them as a string of non sequiturs.

I suppose none of it matters really, except as a vivid and connected landscape inside the head of the boy who watched helplessly. It mattered to me then, and it must have been the complex painfulness of the experience which brought on in me a viral fever later that summer which nearly carried me off like the flies. The dust-storm, in my recollection, came before my fever, so it is likely – if such idle chronology is of any more consequence than the name of a dwarf or the death of a bear – that it raged on that precise evening when the bear man died and the policeman with the huge paunch netted himself and shot that innocent animal.

It was certainly a storm unusually savage. A tumid stillness when no leaf stirred, then a louring sky which made the evening's idle kite-fliers pull back their kites and the Okay Tata trucks pull up at dhabas for milk-brown tea in rudimentary shelter, then shallow gusts which swept the dust along the roads and into eyes, and then suddenly, finally, the full fury recorded in the Pastoral Symphony, the violins and the trumpets and the drums lashing down the gulmohar and the amaltas and the electric poles and the phone lines without quarter.

It made the first page in the papers the next day, which satisfied Abba. But to me it seemed short of being a fulfilment of the Nostradramatic apocalypse predicted by the little tailor next door.

For that I only had to wait a fortnight.

The rains came early that year and over the initial burst it rained for four days without a break. That first stretch of the monsoon was a relief, I remember. God's promise to Noah, as modified to suit our weather pattern, was that it would rain like hell after forty days of miserable heat. Well it did. North India became like Kerala and Venice put together. Since life was a project for Amma, she dug out pictures of Canaletto to show us what our town might become and re-read the truth about Noah from the gospel. But in my book, the fury of the rains that year was connected most centrally with the prophecy made by Nasterji the day the bear was shot.

Every day, in the early monsoon of that year, Abba emerged from the loo to make his matutinal pronouncement on the previous day's rainfall, as though he had something personal to do with its inexorable increase. The only difference now was that Fahrenheit had given way to millimetres. He preferred saying how many millimetres of rain had fallen to centimetres or inches because it sounded more impressive that way, and because he felt his identity swell like a river after he'd said it.

Hundreds of millimetres seemed to fall every day as the monsoon progressed from Assam to Bengal to Bihar to our town in Uttar Pradesh. The Brahmaputra was in spate, the Ganga was rising, the troubled Yamuna chafed underneath her banks, the Narmada had burst her sides, and even the nondescript Gomti had developed an identity of crisis proportions which threatened to spill over into our town.

In mid September it did. Every day there were pictures of army jawans plugging breaches in miscellaneous north Indian rivers, urged on by mimic Nehrus and ministers in white chaprasi caps. But in our town the waters were out to avenge the bear and drown the callousness of the citizens. It was the sort of thing the Old Testament was made up of.

The floods of that year came right up the Jai Kishan Road and bit into the roots of the few gulmohar and amaltas that remained, paving the way for the construction of that area into the middle-class slum it later became. The trees were washed away, and so were all the inhabitants of the road – the cobbler, the cigarette seller, and the water and ice-cream men. I do not think they drowned, though they may have been part of the statistics of death by water which Abba read out to us at our uncle's house, where we'd shifted to tide over the floods. My uncle, as I said, was a very important man. He was in the Indian Administrative Service. His paunch was even bigger than the policeman's and his house was in the safest part of town, uncontaminated by cobblers,

47

cigarette sellers and bear men. It was guarded by an empty sentry box and lay well beyond the reach of the waters.

Masterji and Nasterji left their shop during the flood of that year and came back after the waters had receded and the cholera epidemic had had its season. I was used to their annual absence over the period of Mohurram, when they closed up shop and retreated into their village community somewhere in the remote hinterland beyond Bara Banki. In the year of that flood they had to pull down their shutters a second time, and this time it was for so long that I wondered if they'd drowned in some obscure part of the country which didn't even make it to Abba's newspapers. But in October they were back, and I was relieved to be part of their shop once more, relieved that Nasterji's desperate sense of doom had carried no more threat than Abba's pronouncements each morning.

Over the next few years, Jackson Road slowly changed in character. Landscapes became properties and one by one the bungalows on our road were sold off to people with paunches called developers. Values rose, and so did rents, and as the double-storeyed housing colonies devoured the bungalows like a spreading boa constrictor, the road began to look more and more like its native name which now snaked out of new tongues as Lajwanti Hingorani Chattopadhyaya Marg.

My parents were driven by the prices out of Jackson Road, and my brother and I more indifferently out of Jackson Road or Jai Kishan Road or L.H.C. Marg. We went from there to a cheaper Anglo-Indian locality with a fading colonial ring, Lawrence Terrace, where the name and the price were both acceptable. Stray eucalyptus saplings stood uncertainly near our new flat, wearing a lean and hungry look. No flowers defied the sun below our fly-gauzed windows, which looked eyeball to eyeball at identical windows on either side. We were twenty minutes by rickshaw from our old home. We lived near the Anglo-Indian lady in the Doris Day frock.

Masterji and Nasterji managed to hold on to their little shop and even prospered within the increased congestion and money that came upon their road. Our paths diverged and they grew dim in my memory after we left their part of town. I suppose that sort of loss is inevitable and merely commonplace, and I might never have remembered them again had it not been for a second flood which struck our town eleven years after the first.

I was in Delhi by that time, a full-grown man of a certain height and much gained in weight, when a letter from Amma caused me to recollect those tailors in a spasm of affection and grief which arrived with images of gulmohar and amaltas, the death of the bear man, the shooting of the bear, and that strangely undefined apprehension of a dwarf who had so much significance in my eyes.

> By the way, remember those two tailors who used to live next to us on Jackson Road? –

said the last bit of Amma's letter, all jagged with the affectionate Emily Dickinson dashes that characterized her inner life.

> Well you'll be sorry to hear the little one – your Masterji? or was it Nasterji? I mean Nostradamus – went down it seems in the flood a few days back. Apparently he was being moved out of his shop – which got flooded – with his brother and the boat was quite overloaded, which seems just like these stupid government people who've been organizing the rescues here. – There's a nice poem about floods by that Ezekiel fellow – the poet not the gospel-wallah – called 'The Truth About the Floods' which might be in your library, try and read it. – Apparently they were rowing past our place – No 3 – when the poor little chap had a fit of some kind and keeled right over off the boat – and it seems the boat was so full that nobody could do much to save him and they just watched as he went down! What is this country coming to, I tell you? – as Abba would say. There's just no value to human life left any more. I ran into his brother – the taller chap – yesterday and he gave me the bad news. I was quite upset, he was such a shy fellow – some sort of

heart-attack his brother said. Anyway, that's that I suppose – there's so frustratingly little one can do in the middle of all this furniture shifting and a hundred other things except just feel sorry.

Which reminds me, we're staying on with Dolly Aunty and Bhalloo Uncle for a few more days, until everything gets back to normal, so write back c/o them. The mango season's finally over, even for these exalted IAS-wallahs, and we're reduced to bananas and porridge for breakfast! How your Abba groans every morning over his blessed newspapers.

Wish you were here. Write fast.

Shiploads of love says Abba. – And from me too.

Amma

'Eleven years!' I thought. How quickly they had gone! How distant I had grown from the world of Jai Kishan Road, and yet how easily that letter stripped bare the intervening years and took me back to the late summer of that year, to a house on a road that looked across gulmohar and amaltas to a tailor's shop, to the death of a dwarf, to the flood of houses in which I had lived, rootless as a river.

I folded up the letter and rummaged nostalgically in my bookshelves for *Treasure Island*. A frayed and yellow copy, another fading colour from my past, appeared after a brief hunt.

I pressed Amma's letter carefully into the leaves of that book, as I would a flower.

3

The Othello Complex

It is a truth fortunately rare that a woman in possession of just one husband should produce two unlike sons, one resembling a Greek god and the other a skunk.

It is a tragedy unforgivably singular if you, looking in daily disgust at the mirror on the wall and framing the same nauseating question, are repeatedly informed that your brother looks considerably more desirable than you.

My brother looked even better than Apollo, who we'd seen in our *Illustrated Myths*. For one thing, my brother's eyebrows were nothing like the sun god's. They were a lot heavier, a lot more desirable. You wouldn't have thought it then, when we listened to the sound of a piano by our river which filtered its slow way through the shadows of fading palaces, that my brother's eyebrows would grow to constitute his centre of attraction. But they did. As he grew to manhood I saw them fiercely shade his eyes, giving him that devastating Spartan look. Later, it made the women come in droves to nuzzle up. I closed my eyes and saw them all move their lips, one by one, along the lines of my brother's eyebrows. It was disgusting.

I looked vainly in the mirror for my own resemblance to Apollo, for the women who would come in quietly like ballerinas on tiptoe from the distance behind to soothe my brows. But I seemed specially chosen to resemble one of the higher rodents. On my better days I could have passed off as a rat; when times were hard I barely made it to a racoon.

On one occasion I nearly convinced myself it wasn't true, that only thinking made it so bad. That was when I grew my hair, eked out a stubble, put a Swedish headband round my forehead, clutched a tennis racket and looked in the mirror for Bjorn Borg. He was there. I rushed away to share this triumph with anyone dear who might be near, but Abba, as always, was invisible within the folds of his newspaper world, and I only managed to catch Amma at a bad moment. She was weeping silently over half-cut onions on a chopping board. When she saw Bjorn Borg approach she wiped her eyes, a bit carelessly I thought, to check she wasn't hallucinating. This only seemed to make her more lachrymose and considerably dimmed her view of things. She was looking sneezy and reddish, going on purple, and the movement of my neurons told me the colour purple signified maternal instability. Discretion suggested I either take up the onions on her behalf or escape *molto pronto*; instinct directed me, with customary wisdom, straight to the door. At least, I thought, my physiology was finely tuned and functional.

My failure to look good drove me to a daily bath, so I'd at least smell good. It helped for a few days, till the dog, who I loathed, came up sniffing and gave me a friendly lick. That drove me to poetry. Our mother, who was well-read and sensed the contortions in my psyche, said I was old enough to have a go at Philip Larkin, but the understated global despair which bathed all his nail-on-the-head observations only reminded me of the wonkiness in my own *Weltanschauung* and made my misery deepen like a coastal shelf; I got out of him as early as I could. In the end, a last, careful, forlorn look in the mirror matured me to a sardonic reconciliation. I wasn't Bjorn Borg, nor Clint Eastwood, not even Charles Bronson. My closest famous lookalike was E.M. Forster. There was no more to be said. I had no option except to cultivate the ironic mode and keep the sublimity that swelled up down to a minor key. My self-image was right.

I shrugged what little there was of my shoulders, grimaced in the way that Bjorn Eastwood might after losing a Wimbledon final played out in the Wild West, and retired, like my tennis hero, into a helpless watchfulness. The women would lie in my brother's world; mine lay only inside my head and got mixed up with all sorts of stray images and tunes, the odds and ends that shored me against my racoonic ruin. I resolved upon acquiring the epistemology of a skunk by nosing my way through the world, supplementing this with the ontology of a dachshund by scurrying here and there after my brother. I gave up looking at my brother and myself, and, after an epic inner struggle which got me confused about which bit of me came out victorious, I stopped stroking my eyebrows to thicken their appeal. There were better things to massage in my imagination.

In one of the two houses next door, by the banks of our river, a young Austrian woman, golf-widowed, attempted the 'Appassionata' on an ill-tempered clavier. Her keyboard was an antediluvian Steinway which had soaked in a large portion of the Ganges coming upstream from Calcutta to our city. It sounded bass during the monsoons and treble in the dry season. She, nostalgic for a world that lay far beyond ours, played it every evening all year round, sometimes in concert with the pianists on her long-playing records. At first the melodies seemed alien to us. Then we got used to them and they filtered their way into our circulation, making us whistle in instinctive accompaniment to all her favourite pieces.

She was called Felicia Blumenthal: I should say 'spelt' rather than 'called' because she wrote her name so littered with diacritical marks it required a pronunciation table alongside to make her out. Her speech was similarly accented. She was emphatic about her foreignness, her difference and distance from things Indian. Not that she needed to stress her outlandishness. Her music, the pallor of her skin, and the pastel loveliness of her home amid the garish constructions and the mud huts of our city – all these made her uniqueness palpitatingly clear to my brother and myself.

The simple obsession of our lives in those days was to get

as voyeuristically close as possible to Felicia. Most evenings we managed to watch her unobserved from the shores of the river, where we'd stroll down to feast our eyes on the coolness of the water and the heat halo that radiated out of her bosom and legs. Her Mikimoto pearls swung gently over ebony as she hunched spectacularly over that temperamental Steinway. Her playing soothed our innards, like the mellow movement of yoghurt down the oesophagus; it temporarily enriched our lust with a supplementary feeling which my brother said must be Romantic Love.

Ludwig van Beethoven frowned down at Felicia from where she'd hung him up above her instrument, his chest riddled with the notes of the 'Waldstein' sonata. She liked to infect the unwary with her worship of him, and once showed us nineteen versions of the 'Emperor' Concerto out of her large record collection. She knew we liked her tunes and played that particular concerto for us several times. I found the music suited my biorhythms. It began with a very passionate bang which got me all a-tingle, then it interspersed lots of other impassioned bangs with soothing and fluid melodies. The records had seductively beautiful covers which made me want to look at them, hold them. They went with how I felt about Felicia. I smiled sheepishly in uncomprehending sympathy when she said, once, that her own genealogy only stretched back to Liszt who, she said, gave her great-grandmother music lessons in return for her body. But that wondrous mix of aural and physiological contact seemed only to have been transmitted down the ages as a genetic code which ended up with Felicia like the Lady of Shallott, forlorn and palely tinkling.

We were in our early teens then, and Felicia Blumenthal's fingers seemed to strum at the chords that lay deep within us. Our bodies were on the rise and she, with her impressive and alien pallor, her collection of Emperors and her elegantly stroking fingers, was all we desired. She belonged to a world of music and softness that we craved, mostly because we wanted her so much, but partly I reckoned because she aroused, even within the

54

consuming hardness of our adolescence, a sublimer softness which we inherited from our mother. Music and desire together thickened our blood.

Felicia was married to a Dravidian golfball. He was globular, dark and uniformly pock-marked, and, like all male South Indians, he went by the generic name of Subbu. My brother said he had been a Siberian crane in his previous life, he was so seldom seen. We decided he slept with his putter on a green and expended his nocturnal desires upon the eighteenth hole, looking at pictures of Arnold Palmer and Jack Nicklaus. He was affable enough on the rare occasions we met him, but most days we only woke to the sound of his car disappearing towards the golf-course. We couldn't fathom his devotion to golf with Venus her-self consenting to share his abode, though his lack of interest in her was some consolation against our own distance from her body. We asked our mother about their marriage.

'Felicia suffers from the Othello complex,' said Amma, adding reflectively, 'He loved her for the music that she played, and she loved him that he did listen.' My mother was always adapting Shakespeare to suit her own needs. She had Europe in her bones.

We had to concede the golfball some credit for having dis-covered that the way to Felicia's heart was up her fingers, but it cheered me when our mother reminded us that Othello came to a grisly end. It got me anticipating the time when Subbu would be brained by a flying Aryan golfball, leaving the coast clear for me to marry Felicia and live happily ever after. But there was a huge spoke in my wheel. He lived next door too.

He was called Laurence Corbett and he had no diacritics to his credit. Corbett lived on the other side from Felicia. Like her, he was in his late twenties, but unlike her handicapped husband he was tall, dark and passing handsome. Every time I saw him the same unfailing Americanism came to mind: 'Drat.' Of course I never spoke it out. Amma had a Beethoven frown reserved for everything American except Marlon Brando.

Corbett was about the last Anglo-Indian in India, the others all having become brown with us natives or having escaped, after powdering themselves white, to their utopias in Australia and Canada. We asked our mother how he got so singularly left behind and she said the visa queues to the white world didn't move for dark people.

'There's no need to feel sorry for him though,' she said. 'I believe he's inherited the Corbett money.'

We didn't feel in the least bit sorry for Laurence. He was merely a male and so would normally have been of no more consequence to us than an insect, except for several things – his disgustingly muscular and dusky physiognomy, his potential as a thorn on account of Felicia's Othello complex, his presence as our hated sports teacher in school, and his obscure descent from the writer we most admired, Jim Corbett.

That name, Corbett, had about the same currency in our world as Gandhi and Nehru. At the time that Gandhi and Nehru were shooing out the colonials, Jim Corbett was shooting his way through the country's tiger population, claiming the beasts were all man-eaters. He was Anglo-Indian and had retired from the railways, following up his shunting and hooting years with years of hunting and shooting. It's a fair bet he went about giving the tigers a bad name so he could kill them all for fun, but whatever the truth, he wrote up very many hair-raising man-eater stories that got gobbled up by the million and made him a man of much property. His sole surviving descendant, our neighbour, inherited his ancestor's mantle and his arsenal, in addition to that considerable and undeserved fortune. But he wasn't content to rest, as any sane man would, on his ancestor's laurels. He harried unwilling schoolchildren like us into boxing-rings and made extra money over school holidays by taking foreign tourists on shooting expeditions, using his filthy lucre to beget more filthy lucre. His ambition, by rumour, was to bag a tiger of his own.

Laurence Corbett belonged to the world of hardness we feared and hated. He plagued our blissfully inert lives with compulsory physical activity and dampened our emotional aspirations with the dark and indubitable fact that he existed. I feared and hated him a lot more fiercely than my brother, but I always smiled unctuously at him out of congenital cowardice. Being petrified of even the most minor forms of physical injury, I had no desire to displease Laurence lest he do me bodily harm.

The activity of my imagination assuaged the frequent dullness of my days. I used the weapons of the weak against Corbett and got even with him in my mind. My favourite nocturnal fantasy which didn't feature Felicia was the one in which I commanded Laurence to accompany me as my coolie on a tiger-shoot. I sauntered calmly ahead, he followed gasping, too terrified of me to curse the overload on his head and shoulders. As Amma once said in a more sympathetic context, in India the white man's burden had to be borne by the Anglo-Indian.

When we reached the forests where Hunter dispatches Fearful Symmetry back to the blacksmith who forged him for the pleasure of the hunt, I discovered I'd forgotten to bring the goat which would serve as bait to lure in our man-eating tiger. I blamed this on Laurence, of course, cursing his stupidity and giving him a few kicks for good measure, making him cower where all self-respecting coolies cower: in the background. Naturally the hunt, being an activity divinely ordained, could not be abandoned for mere lack of a goat: the Anglo-Indian would have to serve instead. As my mother might have said, adapting some irrelevant poet or other to present exigency, they also serve who only lie as bait.

I trussed up the last surviving descendant of Jim Corbett like a spring chicken, then scattered a whole lot of spring onions all over him to make it a salad day for the incoming tiger.

'This way the tiger will know he has to spring on you, Laurence,' I said with a wicked chuckle, carefully inserting a couple of spring onions into his nostrils.

Laurence did not seem in the least bit amused. He snorted, dislodging one of my spring onions. It emerged with a bit of goo, so I had to replace it rather gingerly, without soiling my fingers.

His initial grovelling had degenerated into a most unaesthetic variety of abuse in Hindi, which unnecessarily brought my mother and non-existent sister into the picture – the dominance of the mother figure in our country is prone to make the Indian male Oedipally complexed, as seemed manifest from Laurence's very un-Anglo-Indian vocabulary. To quieten him down, I was forced to place my last spring onion within his mouth, so that he might lie in wait for the tiger feeling bitterly supine.

I myself shinnied up, much like Tarzan, to the extempore tree-house I had so skilfully constructed, following the example of Laurence's forefather, who had the good sense to shoot all his tigers sitting safely cocooned in a machaan, several feet beyond the mightiest leap ever recorded for a tiger. I fell asleep in that dark and womb-like enclosure: it made me feel handsome and secure, and safe from the travails to which sensitive people like us are so subject in this mighty universe of ours. I woke briefly to the sound of a man-eater scrunching his way through spring onion and bone. I snuggled deeper into my pillow, smiling with cathartic satisfaction at the poetic justice, late achieved, of feeding the last Corbett to a man-eater.

The trouble was really that, as Hamlet said to Horatius while defending the bridge, there were more things between heaven and earth than could be made to perish by one's philosophy, the chiefest among these being El Corbett. Laurence Corbett's existence was as inescapable and real as my resemblance to Clint Eastwood was not, and his proximity made me quiver with a feeling of profound physical vulnerability. So did Felicia. The difference was that Laurence Corbett was all I did not desire.

One day Felicia came by to borrow some tomatoes and was speaking to our mother in that voice straight out of Lauren Bacall's stomach. We hung about to sneak in some soulful looks at her legs, and at whatever else might become visible if by some miracle she had to bend. Our tactility was very alight, making us all soft and speechless. Our mother made up for us. She had once sung in the Amen Chorus of Handel's *Messiah* and studied English Literature, so Felicia considered her a soul-mate in the great heart of darkness which was our city, and bared her life in the spasms of neighbourliness that are aroused when one comes to borrow tomatoes.

They were chattering happily when our pet lapdog nosed his way into the kitchen and gave Felicia's leg a lick, making her bend to pick him up and pat him fondly. Every dog has his day, said our fluttering hearts, after the paroxysms ceased.

Felicia's affection for dogs gave me an idea.

'Why don't we take the dog to her place sometime?' I suggested to my brother. 'She'll want to stroke him.'

'What's the good of that?' asked my brother. 'He'll have all the fun and won't know it. How 'bout getting her to stroke *us* instead?'

'That's the general idea ya,' I said. 'You wait and see.'

My brother shrugged his muscular shoulders. I twitched mine in painful imitation. But for a change I was going to hold the leash.

All pet dogs in India in those days were called either Tiger or Caesar, regardless of sex. Their function in life was sensibly dogly – to guard houses night and day, preferably on no food at all, so that their bark and bite might achieve an equal ferocity. Our dog was different. He was a runt of a Pekinese with little bark and no bite who'd been spoilt by affection. Our mother fed him a *haute cuisine* which weighed twice as many milligrams as he did, and, on account of her perverse immersion in things theatrical, she named him after a villain in Shakespeare. My passionate feelings of sibling rivalry, laid latent against my brother after much inner strife, got directed against Iago every time my mother fed him a cheese soufflé or a chocolate mousse. There, into that overgrown earthworm, I thought, goes my food again and again. It was revolting.

I tried to think up a plan that would kill two birds with one stone, getting a feel of Felicia and getting cathartically even with the dog. My brother, all benign and rippling, was sceptical and content to do the watching.

So, the next evening, hearing Amma safely crooning her base version of Schubert's 'Ave Maria' under the shower, I borrowed a bone from the fridge and went off to lie in wait by the river. For a change I wasn't idly hoping Iago would drown: suddenly even he had a use. I tantalized him with the bone till he was in a state of high frenzy, then soothed him into thinking he was about to get the bone, then tantalized him again into a slavering hysteria for the meat.

This sort of torture requires much intellectual precision. You have to know exactly how far you can play Tantalus-cum-Torquemada without letting the dog get depressed into losing faith in his own ability *vis-à-vis* the bone. You can more or less gauge a dog's IQ by how long he takes to lose interest in a hunk of meat cooingly offered and then systematically denied. Paradoxically, the stupider the dog the longer he exercises himself in the manner of female Romanian gymnasts on a balancing beam, jumping endlessly towards the impossible. I was the world expert on this variety of Pavlovian torture and could keep Iago going like a yo-yo almost endlessly: you could see that from the expression of disgust on my brother's face and the snarl on the dog's.

All this stopped when I heard Felicia cease hammering her clavier: her post-hammerclavier period was always a gentle stroll in the garden, which sloped down to the river.

I gave Iago one last sniff at the bone and threw it carefully in the direction Felicia was likely to take. Iago rushed off after the bone; I rushed off after Iago with feigned fury, as though trying strenuously to prevent him violating the boundaries of her house, all the while composing my features to give out a red-skinned mixture of apology, outrage and helplessness in the face of canine lunacy.

Sure enough, Felicia was astroll in a gratifyingly mini sort of outfit which gave away her legs and some other good bits above the belt. Iago appeared with his bone safely in his mouth. I envied him his meat.

'Terribly sorry Felicia,' I said, 'the dog seems to have spotted something in your garden and got away before I could stop him.'

I grinned cravenly by way of neighbourly apology, picking up Iago with a rough sort of lunge to indicate masterly annoyance.

'Oh,' said Felicia, 'I thought you were making him chase his bones towards my garden.'

Her Austrian pedigree gave an interesting turn to her English syntax, and another sort to my stomach. I was wondering how to frame a reply that would create subtle confusion, enabling a change of topic, but to my relief Felicia wasn't being at all accusatory. She smiled benignly and I smiled back nervously, petting and smacking Iago to indicate a transition to fond annoyance, getting in a couple of hasty looks at her cleavage in the process. Sufficient unto the day was the joy thereof. It was a lot better than my brother'd ever managed.

I was emboldened. She was so near, and yet, as my mother would have said, a man's reach exceeds his grasp – which inane bit of poetic sagacity would have meant just the same to me if it had been framed the other way round.

'Nice evening though,' I said, venturing a non sequitur that might give me another few seconds of stolen glimpse.

'Oh yes,' she said, 'November is my most favourite season.'

'So's mine,' I said. 'November is definitely my most favourite season too.'

'You see,' I added, blundering on joyously and with light-headed anarchism, 'I was born in November, and ever since then it has been my most favourite season.'

'Ah,' said Felicia, looking a bit mystified.

I knew there was something wrong in what I'd said the moment after I'd said it, as frequently happens when Man is confronted with Woman, but the blunder wasn't of the insuperable sort. In fact, I thought, a little confusion was just right. It allowed me to hang on a further few seconds, and, if I didn't overstep my tongue, it might even miraculously lead on to the bower of wedded bliss. I was already seeing this as our First Real Meeting.

'December's not bad either,' I said, 'though it's a bit cold for us.'
'Hm.'

'You see,' I said more confidentially, 'as Indians we aren't really used to the cold. But you as an Austrian must be used to the cold.'
'Hm.'

Two 'hms' are just about companionable; a third might have made me feel crowded out.

'It must be quite cold in Austria,' I added quickly, frantically searching my surcharged cells for further information on Austria. They sent me back the Blue Danube.

'The Danube,' I said with a slow reflectiveness which I hoped she'd recognize as profundity, 'must certainly turn blue with the cold.'

She laughed most prettily at that, making me feel uneasily triumphant at having parried away another 'hm,' and at getting time to switch off the weather. My neurons had just about compiled a hasty list of composers for me to start blabbing about, beginning with Allegri and ending in Zymanowski, when she began slowly strolling, as if to say she'd see me down to the river. I followed a step behind, in the manner of a dutiful Hindu wife, though for better reason – it gave a good view from the rear.

'Oh,' she said, after two steps (which let me see both her two legs), 'I forgot to take off this necklace. I wear it for my piano-playing only.' She raised her arms to undo her pearls and got me nearly into a swoon at the sight of her armpits. In my delirious haze I saw a lucky Jesus swinging dangerously down her neck at the bottom of a slim golden chain.

'Oh,' she said again, 'the clasp of this stupid necklace has got stuck.'

I swallowed hard as a preliminary to digesting this gift from God.

Now, I ask you, lives there a man, *any* man, who calls himself man, who has not dreamed this most innermost of all dreams, where his Immortal Beloved comes into the garden, strolls awhile apace with him, stops with a feminine start, says she must unclasp herself, fails prettily after exposing armpits, and, after a final and most becoming hesitation, asks him to undo her, with a blush?

I don't remember how I unclasped that clasp, my fingers were trembling so bad, but I remember it involved, first, dropping Iago with a thud, second, touching Felicia's neck for at least two seconds, and third, hearing something that sounded like an epileptic fit from the direction where I reckoned my brother was stationed.

'Thank you,' she said, laughing most becomingly, just like the One in my dreams. My index, middle and ring fingers got a one-point-five-second touch as I handed over the goods. Felicia dripped the necklace into a mini-pocket.

'Iago likes November too,' I said, trying a new line to stave off the Death of Parting. 'He hates the summer and the monsoon because of the ticks. I'm sure he'd be happy in your country. There couldn't be too many ticks there, are there?'

She laughed and looked at the dog, but didn't bend to pet him. I wasn't desperately disappointed. After the unclasping, my feelings had been transformed from lust to love, a sort of impassioned Platonism and once the soul comes into the picture, one does not mind quite as much if the object of one's desire fails to reveal herself instantly and continuously.

This was the right time for the master plan. I picked up Iago with a nonchalant sort of swoop, scratching around his ticks to keep him soothed and unstruggling.

'He's quite a friendly dog really and doesn't mind being petted by anyone,' I said, letting out the hint. 'Not like other dogs,' I said, by way of reinforcing the suggestion.

'Oh yes,' she said, looking affectionately at the villain. That was good enough to bring the second stage into play.

I moved my left hand towards Iago's throat and let my right take his hindermost, stroking him kindly with the fingers of both and throttling him now and then, until he dropped the bone from his mouth in disgust. I smiled and smiled to offset Iago's expression, remembering with some discomfort the bardic view that one may smile and smile and be a very villain.

'Here Felicia, you can stroke him a bit if you like,' I said.

That sentence was constructed along a careful syntax. It had to sound, for authenticity, as though I was doing her the favour, that she couldn't stroke my dog as long as she liked, but only as long as I was pleased to let her. By this time my facial muscles, all eager to please, were working overtime towards that primal, dedicated stare by which the natural hero deposits his soul into the beloved; regrettably the outcome, on that occasion, was something akin to a hideous grin, because Felicia merely smiled palely and stroked the dog under his chin.

This was a momentary blow, but unmomentous for one who knew not vanquishment or defeat. I edged my left hand imperceptibly forward and stroked Iago too, pretending to keep my fingers carefully distant from her area of the dog but actually letting them stray cautiously into her territory. It worked pretty well and our fingers touched casually several times, slightly diluting my love back towards lust, but without seriously impairing either emotion.

It was going well for me thus, and who knows how many more seconds it might thus have gone on going well for me, had there not been a loud 'Hullo' heard from the other side, where Laurence Corbett lived. That was probably the first time in my life I actually uttered the word 'drat': Laurence Corbett had clambered over the low wall and was sauntering over towards the Happy Couple and Dog, not so much with neighbourly bonhomie and goodwill as with an aura of masculine assurance, the way I knew Man must walk when approaching Woman.

The absolute philosophical disjunction between my dream world, where Corbett had been consumed by a man-eater, and reality, where he approached with fearful symmetry to eat into my own flesh and blood, felt like a hit below the belt. To my despair, Felicia looked all aflutter and reciprocal. She stopped fondling Iago and forgot about me. Her skin took on a different

64

glow. She undripped the pearls from her pocket and, with the skill of practised fingers, hooked them gracefully round her neck again, suppressing Jesus once more.

That simple gesture made me feel as inconsequential as an insect. It made me want to go rushing back to my mother, to my brother, to a hole in the ground where I might crawl in and die. It spoke out a whole world of feeling, undoing all the constructions of my mind, all the tremble that my fingers had known, all the love and lust I ever felt for anything. The music and desire that mingled in my own being for her were now reflected outwards from her body, at the intruder who strode so casually and confidently towards the regions of my happiness. In all the years that I had lived, in all the time I had spent cultivating the ironic mode to keep my features safely distant from my emotional life, I had never before felt so completely helpless.

Felicia's eyes gleamed a welcome to Corbett and I knew, looking at the exalted sort of radiance she gave out, what my mother meant when she said that Felicia suffered from the Othello complex. It was one of life's great mysteries to me that she, who belonged to the world of softness and music and could distinguish between nineteen versions of the 'Emperor' Concerto, could suffer so badly from a biological pull which allowed Laurence Corbett into her world with such carefree and naked ease, so completely without strategy and master plan. It was the first time Reality kicked me as hard as that, making me understand the value of a life free of vulnerability and dreams.

I dropped Iago with a thud. He hadn't a chance in life. Nor, I thought, had Subbu; it made me less sceptical about his fondness for living out his life in bunkers. Watching Corbett and Felicia that day, and sensing the clicking of chemistry between brown muscle and white skin, my premonition was that the future lay in wait only for my brother.

Corbett and Felicia had reached the low boundary which scarcely separated them from each other. My house lay in the opposite direction. I walked towards it and away from Felicia, towards my brother and my world, where affection and the culti-vation of an ironic selfhood shored me against my romantic, racoonic ruin.

It was, on the surface, a peaceful and undramatic evening, with a gentle breeze ruffling the water, when my brother sat by our river while it filtered a slow path through the shadows of fading palaces, watching in suppressed silence as I tried out my hand in a world that lay so near and yet so remote from our own.

As for me, I had come as close as I ever would to immortal bliss. It was time for me to get back to being my brother's keeper.

4

Death by Music

'If suicide wasn't such a permanent thing,' said my brother, 'I'd commit it once a day. Some days maybe twice.' I wasn't surprised. He was looking at film magazines which had pictures of Elizabeth Taylor. She did not suffer from the Othello complex. But where was she?

The cup of my brother's life brimmed over with a shallow wit. As I said, we looked quite different from each other, he magnificent like Zeus and later Beethoven, I like E.M. Forster, but he felt the same way as me; every time we saw beautiful women the injustice of life came home to us and, like Hamlet, we weighed the pros and cons of doing ourselves in. A battle between desire and death raged within us all the time.

Looking at those pictures and gauging our impossible distance from Hollywood, I agreed with my brother, though I knew that on other days, when the blues hadn't struck with their habitual ferocity, life seemed tolerably liveable, occasionally even ecstatic. It was that oscillation between feeling traumatically low and excitedly high which sank me in gloom, making me sceptical about living out life with an emotional gas regulator, always checking on how much feeling to let flow, how high to keep the flame without burning other people or burning out, how much of myself to express without feeling vulnerable, exposed, misunderstood.

Of course we weren't serious about suicide, desisting out of fear of pain: my brother said Hamlet's problem with suicide wasn't that it was unaesthetic but that he didn't have an anaesthetic. It would certainly have hurt to pass into a realm where one couldn't even savour apple tart the next day. In some vague way we felt there lay ahead of us a future pregnant with possibilities. Our palate for what it held in taste for us dampened the desire for self-slaughter, and so the native hue of resolution was sicklied o'er with the pale cast of a proven pudding. Desire won the day; death might have seemed acceptable if it didn't cut us off so dismayingly from the senses, or if it took us off painlessly to some undiscovered country from whose bourne no traveller returns.

'Hey man, put on the "Emperor" Concerto,' said my brother, scattering the magazines all over the bed.

'Okay,' I said. I opened our record box and put Beethoven's 'Emperor' Concerto on the record-changer.

In those adolescent days, when life seemed a balancing beam between perdition at one end and orgasm at the other, music served in some ways as a ready-to-hand substitute for sex. My brother and I had immunized ourselves against the impossibilities of lust and intimations of mortality with Beethoven's 'Emperor' Concerto, in which the melodies seemed to give sufficient form to all the feelings we had ever harboured. Earlier, I had fretted awhile over the words to choose in some stupendous literary endeavour to transform soulful torment into aesthetic torrent, but the flow of my phrases got nowhere near the tunes in the 'Emperor' Concerto. There was an immense, impassioned, ordered turbulence about that music which set in perspective everything else in life and made it seem the highest cathartic interruption within the general desirability of silence.

Not that it was possible to get away from desire. Even the act of putting on that music had a faintly sexual tinge. Our record-changer had an erect metallic obelisk wedged into the centre of a rotating disk. The record sat on this Cleopatric needle for a few seconds and then, with a subtle bit of foreplay, the needle nudged the record right down its firm length, onto the rotator. Now it was time for the record-changer to use its arm: it had a phallic arm with a gentle curve and a hard tip. For a few seconds that arm hovered in the air, as though searching an entrance, and then gently but firmly it closed in over the 'Emperor' Concerto. As that diamond tip nestled into the opening groove and the orchestra came alive with a triumphant orgasmic crash, we felt our veins flood with the sound of salvation. We closed our eyes and felt our bodies embrace something as sweet as Elizabeth Taylor.

'Lower the volume for God's sake,' yelled Amma from her bedroom. We paid no heed and she came in storming. 'For God's sake,' she said, softening the 'Emperor' and closing the magazines full of Liz Taylor, 'can't you boys do anything better with your lives than mooning around filmstars?'

'Elizabeth Taylor is my birthright,' said my brother firmly, 'and I shall have her.'

Amma raised an eyebrow, angling her disdain in our general direction. In her hierarchy neither plastic film nor orchestrally manufactured sound could surpass the hum of domestic contentment. She knew the difference between illusion and reality and patted each into its proper place, smoothing their creases. She clicked mostly to the music of knitting needles, which communicated present tranquillity and future warmth. My brother and I took the sounds of domestic bliss for granted; we were in search of the exotic and the extraordinary.

'I had a dream recently,' he explained, 'a very strange one. I dreamt I was playing the lyre in Sparta, near Mount Olympus, and out of the blue who should come walking down to me but Elizabeth Taylor, arm in arm with Zeus.'

'I'm surprised,' said Amma smiling. 'Are you sure she wasn't arm in arm with you?' She walked off towards the reality of her cushions, which needed to be tidied, and the music of her whistling pressure-cooker.

My brother explained the rest of his convoluted dream to me, a happy frolicsome dream which contrived to pull together so many of the images which rotated like planets upon the disk of our sun-god minds. In his dream my brother attempted the sweet violence of the 'Emperor' Concerto on the lower tones of his antique instrument, and the nobility of this ridiculous effort, spotted by Zeus, made the god so full of mirth that in a fit of magnanimity he offered to make Paris out of my brother as reward for his next life, when he could have Helen all to himself and sway to the rhythms of her dance in all the Hindi films that ever came out of Bombay.

But my brother, desiring his companion Elizabeth Taylor instead, was intemperately changed into a Golden Retriever by the irate god, being retrieved from a canine end only by the divine intervention of Miss Taylor, who liked Golden Retrievers. One day, with Zeus asnooze, she disguised one of her hundred husbands as Achilles, then asked him to take the kennel and fling it with all his might, dog and all, into the River Gomti, which filtered unnoticed through the shadows of fading palaces, past the obscurest town in all Asia, where Zeus would never look. She also ordained that before the kennel fell upon the river it would change its form to a basket made of bulrushes anxiously awaited by a horde of barren washerwomen, all in search of forlorn babies which might float past their river in baskets made of bulrushes. When the women had done killing themselves over this scarce resource, the only survivor among them, after drowning the rest along the prescribed rules of Indian capitalism, would find inside a musical baby with hearing so perfect he would be the envy of Ludwig van Beethoven when he was full-grown. To this full-grown inheritor of the 'Emperor' Concerto, declared my brother, Elizabeth Taylor had made it known that she would some day return. 'And if I remember the whole dream right,' he said, 'she's going to arrive in the shape of a queen. Yes, that's right, she'll come like an empress.'

The level of anarchy in that dream somehow faded out of our bodies as we grew older, but in those days it made perfect sense to me. That dream seemed a premonition, or the articulation of an exciting possibility, or at worst a sensuous alchemy of exaltation and despair which found symbolic form in that strange pairing of 'Emperor' and empress. The incredible harmony of tempestuous impulse and quiet sadness which moved within the grooves of the 'Emperor' Concerto seemed linked, with an eccentricity which fortified us against the inequities of life, with the always restless, always mobile, forever beautiful form of Elizabeth Taylor.

Something of this same restless, questing, searching feeling lay in the ample bosom of Elizabeth Taylor as she stepped out of the cinema screen of the Delite Talkies, leaving Mark Antony, Octavius Caesar and a swimming pool of asses' milk to play out the rest of *Cleopatra*.

It was perhaps a fortnight after that dream. My brother and I were part of a normal, sexually-repressed crowd of fellow natives watching the late show of that film in our small city theatre, when she calmly detached herself from tinsel and celluloid, stepped into our little movie hall, walked down the four wooden steps that separated the screen from the audience, and came straight towards our seats.

There were perhaps five hundred people in the audience, all erotically hungry for Elizabeth Taylor. English movies had begun giving way to the Hindi cinema, and the crowds only paid money to watch Hollywood heroines if they knew they were getting sex in return for their investment. 'Strictly for Adults', the tag attached to *Cleopatra*, partly betokened the censor board's antediluvian notion of sex – which was a white woman who revealed anything between her neck and her knees – but mostly it served to draw in the throngs. In our town that label usually brought in every man to leer awhile and return home cheered.

News had got around that there were juicy titbits in *Cleopatra* which involved some queen floating about in a semi-transparent pool of milk, so a full house watched the film eagerly, hoping the milk in Egypt was as diluted as in India, at least enough to reveal the erogenous zones of a Nubian empress. Sitting like fences in the middle were other voyeurs, namely my brother and me, who had one foot in Los Angeles and the other at home. It was a motley crew that lay in wait for burnished gold to barge Cleopatra into view.

We hadn't bargained for her barging into contemporary India in a debut quite as casually spectacular as this.

'Hello,' she said softly, 'd'you think I can squeeze in somewhere for a bit?'

'Sure, Cleopatra,' I replied coolly in her own sort of Hollywood drawl to aid instantaneous comprehension, 'you c'n sit right here between us.' The arm-rest between my brother and me seemed to have vanished with her appearance, and she squeezed between us to watch the rest of the movie.

Naturally, we waited for the hall to erupt in pandemonium with her entry. But to our amazement the consternation which ensued from her caesura out of ancient Egypt was visible only on screen; there seemed not the slightest evidence of it in our theatre. We looked this way and that, we rubbed our eyes and adjusted our vision, but no change of focus followed. Cleopatra sat beside us, watching what would happen next in *Cleopatra*, apparently invisible to our fellow watchers.

The movie was still running, except Mark Antony and Octavius Caesar were no longer antagonists; they had come close to each other and were looking aghast in our general direction. For some reason, which I saw as their lack of vision, they couldn't see beyond the screen which separated them from us; their world lay in illusion. Behind them we saw a slowly gathering herd of asses alongside an army of extras. The asses brayed vigorously in our direction before wandering off-screen to waste their snorts upon the desert air. The extras scratched themselves here and there, accustoming their bodies to the fact that in such sandy climes even a substantial woman might prove a mirage and just thinly vanish.

We watched the movie hypnotized, held in thrall by what was happening. Yet only my brother and I seemed to see that the woman who sat near us, all scented and Oriented, smiling at the bewilderment of her co-stars on screen, was the missing

Cleopatra. Age had not withered her, nor husbands staled her infinite desirability. If it wasn't Elizabeth Taylor sitting by our side, it could only be her ideal Platonic form come straight out of the shadowy world of Hollywood.

Meanwhile the movie was running on, perplexing us with new evidence on the decline of the Roman empire. An odd fate seemed to have struck the emperors into an open-mouthed and paralysed inertia uncharacteristic of that period of swashbuckling Roman history. Caesar, Antony, the asses, the extras, were all searching diffidently about them, and it was soon clear to our theatre audience that the missing object of their phallic gaze was Cleopatra.

'Hey Caesar,' shouted Mark Antony, 'does she know how to swim?'

Caesar looked in alarm at the pool of milk. Four little donkeys joined him and stared down too, moved by a different intention. They bent their heads and began lapping up the pool.

'Maybe she's down there somewhere,' said Caesar, now frenzied.

More donkeys crowded around the pool, and soon there was a whole circle of asses drinking up the bath. In a minute it was quite drained, but there was no African queen at the bottom. The crowd had paid good money to see Cleopatra emerge in the nude and patiently awaited her return on their investment.

But to little profit. The passionate international relationship between Rome and Egypt remained, unfortunately for the investors, material for future speculation. For, just at this crucial juncture of history, there was a blackout.

It was an electricity failure, organized specially by all state governments in India to keep citizens in mind of exactly which set of pussy-stroking political villains were currently in power. In the theatre everyone groaned in one go, for the energy required to keep the illusion alive was at least temporarily at an end. The exit lights glowed brighter and several shrill wolf-whistles – directed from the audience at the film operators to get their generator going – got no response at all. People were stirring irritably in their seats, wondering what was going on, exasperated by the emptiness of the pool and the capricious twists of history, and then by the film's frustrating cut before the empress with no clothes could reveal all. But everyone seemed oblivious of the most obvious truth, that Cleopatra had appeared and was now one of us.

'Excuse me,' said Cleopatra to us, loud and clear in the encompassing penumbra, 'could you direct me to a hotel anywhere downtown, if there's one near here, maybe?'

My brother was still adjusting his eyesight but I, though a bit obtuse, was readier with high sentence.

'Sure, Liz,' I said 'we c'n show you some reel cool places downtown.' I spoke as though those words had lodged within me all my life, awaiting only the appearance of a nubile empress to shape my utterance.

'Gee thanks, honey,' she said. 'Let's go then,' she said more urgently, as we shuffled out to the sound of louder wolf-whistles in the diminishing dark. I looked nervously about, certain they were directed at the two of us and Cleopatra, certain they'd stop her leaving with us and put her back on screen to get their money's worth when the generator got going. But no one closed in upon us, no one seemed to see us, and I realized like a one-eyed man that in the country of the blind people see only as much as they are allowed by the shared social vision which constitutes each man's cornea.

As we moved out of the Delite Talkies I saw her ruffle her hair and put a hanky to her eyelids, which she vigorously wiped, and there lay the rub – she seemed to know she couldn't be seen. The liquefaction of her clothes, in which she flowed with us to the foyer, attracted no comment either, even though what she wore was as flamboyantly outlandish as some of the things I'd seen on many of the Anglo-Indian Sandras and Teresas who went arm in arm and cheap high heels down Lovers Lane or the Shahnajaf Road.

Outside the hall, on the M.G. Road which blackened every

Indian town as a memorial to Mahatma Gandhi's abbreviated life, rickshawallahs huddled meagrely on their enlarged tricycles and a paanwallah's rope burnt its slow way towards a swimming pool of betel leaf and white lime.

We made our way through faceless throngs towards the diurnal round of parked rickshaws, the skeletons on them crying out in the dark to attract our custom. My brother and I directed her with complete confidence now, caring nothing, while Cleopatra followed where we led. We would normally have walked to our house, only a mile away, but had telepathically decided that travel with Cleopatra would be more pleasantly tactile, at least for us, if we squeezed into a rickshaw.

There were several people about. Two pregnant men approaching labour scratched their scrotae and had developed white moustaches eating Tootie Frooties. A Bengali gent clutched the tail of his dhoti and repeatedly insulted the nearest wall with vermilion spittle. Jesus, hoist with his own petard on the church steeple opposite, felt helplessly cross carrying the weight of avian multitudes which gurgled and crowned his nest of thorns. Below him university criminals roamed in small bands, combing their hair and then the streets for passing women. A pavement loudspeaker with a sore throat, long devoid of song, screeched its undirected abuse of music alongside the local Come September Brass Band, which brayed encouragement to a three-piece groom already astride his nag. Skeletons plied aimless rickshaws and a South Indian lady, buying a flower garland, whispered to her husband, 'Do you think that was cent per cent donkey milk in which she would be taking her bath?' They all saw straight through Cleopatra, looking at us briefly but seeing nothing amiss.

We knew where to take her, naturally. Every American who ever visited our small town was on his way to a tiger, just as in Africa they were all hunting for their roots. We knew exactly where, within our little urban jungle, she might find what she was looking for.

'Excuse me, Miss Cleopatra,' said my brother, 'we can drop you off at a hotel near here which is quite nice, if you like.'

'You c'n call me Liz,' she said, so we gave her our names, and fishing in her dress pocket she added: 'Sure, any place you c'n recommend should do for now, s'long as it's kinda quiet and large and if they'll take dollars.'

We were getting on quite well, I thought, and wondered at her lack of nervousness, hopping off screen and on to a rickshaw with her first two men in a strange city. I guessed she was a traveller, like the two of us, and felt at home being always on the move. I sensed in particular the affinity between my brother and her from the air of ease they both radiated, from that capacity some people have to appear equally relaxed among schoolchildren or lawyers, golfers or historians, strangers or friends, in the most odd or unlikely circumstances. Even in that short space I had intimations that something of my brother lay in Elizabeth Taylor too, a shared impulse which drove her all that distance from pyramid and sand dune to the obscurest theatre in all Asia.

But the precise contours of a symmetry which linked her world and ours only became obscurely clear to me towards the end of her stay in our town.

All the obvious questions crowded our minds as we huddled into the rickshaw and a skeleton stood on his pedals to move us towards the Jim Corbett Hotel, where a stuffed tiger with permed coat and waxed moustaches glared out a reception from his glass case at the entrance door. How had she made her appearance? Why had she come here, of all places? Was it really true that she sat ensconced between us, being pulled on a rickshaw so soon after rolling out of a rug to a concert of emperors? What was going to happen now? Would she stay awhile or return like a mirage to the screen?

There were so many questions to ask that to ask one or the other seemed futile. There were likely to be so many answers, and all so confusing to our emotions, that silence seemed the most obvious and desired condition of being. We stayed quiet, and so did Liz, warming to each other in the solitude of that shared cold air through the slowly passing sights, the yowl of stray dogs against the temperature, the whiff of open rubbish dumps mingling with the scent of burning eucalyptus where three men crouched to hide a glow.

We were now at the tail end of a straining spine, wondering how it managed to heft three substantial people so lavishly clad. It deserved a thousand dollars, I thought, so it could get itself some warm skin from the morgue. Watching all the absent muscle as that cadaver moved us in the direction of the Jim Corbett Hotel was like taking in an anatomy lesson. His bones were clanking and gleamed white with the oil that dropped down to keep them from rusting. But our sympathy for him was finite; we disembarked at the Jim Corbett Hotel.

The taxidermic tiger gaped at the arrival of Elizabeth Taylor to his hotel, his incisors gleaming at her as though awaiting his dentist. Fortunately he made no other move to receive us, and while my brother haggled with our rickshawallah we waited near the reception desk, at a cautious distance from his excessive fangs. I watched my brother bargain with some embarrassment on account of Cleopatra's obvious concern for the pedaller. Socially, we were always under great pressure never to give anything to beggars, lepers, corpses and the poor, lest the sin of richness deny them the kingdom of heaven, and so that we could spend all we saved on Tootie Frootie and Kassata ice cream. I tried telepathy and got through. He gave the rickshawallah a thousand dollars, which was the new currency of our country, and the bones cycled away saying salaam.

There was no one behind the reception desk. We rang an electric bell which broadcast a low whine and two cockroaches. The cockroaches had their antennae out in alarm but retreated into the bell after giving some thought to our circumstances. No one else appeared. We rang and rang again, but it little profits a hotel rich in vermin to employ receptionists.

'Mebbe they're full up, d'you think?' said Liz finally. 'Can we try someplace else?'

My brother ran after the pedalling silhouette to re-engage his services, and we hopped on once more.

'We live just round the corner from here,' said my brother. 'With our mother,' he added, to suggest she was safe with us.

'We could go home and you could stay overnight in our mother's room, if that's okay by you.'

'Okay,' said Cleopatra with an imperial smile, 'if that's okay with your mama.'

Above us I saw the bounty of the night sky, thick with the loneliness of satellites and the still rain of stars. A moon which had lost its memory was getting nowhere, aimlessly benign, drifting with a happy purposelessness which my brother would emulate more and more as the years passed. I too was happy then, journeying in the dark with my brother and a star, the country emptied of people and an aura of vast spaces from the Milky Way seeping like an adagio through my hormones and my bones.

Through the dream of the moon's unwatchful glow we soon reached home. We had no doubt that Amma, after the initial shock, wouldn't refuse a night's shelter to our stray Cleopatra at that hour of the night. But she surprised us with her perspicacity, saying she was expecting this all along, and merely scolded Cleopatra for being out so late and out of date.

'A girl your age ought to know better than to be gallivanting about at this time of night with these two,' she said. 'I knew these brats would bring you home one day, but I thought you'd be here much earlier.'

We knew she wasn't really upset, of course, recognizing the obliqueness of her affection from the timbre of her scolding. She'd already left Cleopatra her second-best bed, and towel, soap and nightie for the nonce.

Falling asleep on my pillow I remembered asking Amma once how the emperor Babur, walking thrice around the bed of his sick son Humayun, took the disease upon himself.

'I can't tell you how,' Amma replied, adding one of her parables. 'Some things just happen and it's best to take them as they come. Edison said Let there be Light, and there was.'

I awoke the next morning as usual to the opening crescendo of the 'Emperor' Concerto, proclaiming the triumph with which it makes sense to start the superhuman endeavours of each new day. I liked silence in the early mornings and Amma liked bed-tea, but my brother had hegemonized us both into waking up to that music. Liz was still there. She was awake too, alert and listening, which was conclusive proof for us that she hadn't been pulling the rug over our eyes.

'I need a break,' she was telling Amma through Klemperer's majestic conducting. 'I'm through with playing Cleopatra. 'Fact I'm through with playing this queen, that queen, all the time. Gimme a break I said to all those men. Men, men, men, day and night. Makes me sick. Have you noticed how there only seem to have become more and more men and then some in the world lately? Anyhow, I just need a break. I'm through with moving beds and roles and husbands, the whole lot. I need a break. I'm looking for something different, and maybe that something's brought me here.' She paused, searching for some clearer definition of her restlessness, then shrugged.

Amma was the eternal mother and understood the emotional fatigue of continuous travel. We did too, having moved restlessly from one thing to another, unsure of what we searched, certain only of the need to persist in always seeking something other than what we possessed, distrusting the immobility of comfort and accepting instead an unquenchable wanderlust which moved us towards periods of short-lived exhaustion and defined the way we were. We saw Liz as one of us and accepted her presence in our home, refusing to ask the obvious questions and taking it for granted that her visit was something both she and we wanted, or needed, or that was mysteriously but happily fated for us. Her instinctive need was to feel free to say only as much as she wished.

Two days' rest cleared some of the cobwebs in her mind. She said she had felt imprisoned for ages by men, relationships, routine, and the omniscient clamour of human beings, and one day, when it all got too much and she felt herself at the edge of suicidal despair, she thought she saw in front of her eyes a solitary grave where a tree rose out of the earth in the shape of an upturned woman, an image of overpowering beauty towards which she had taken some sort of plunge, finding herself there-after seated in spacious comfort, and assured of movement towards an area of blissful solitude, space and silence. She couldn't recollect anything more, no more than a child recollects its plunge into the world, nor no more than does a transformed Golden Retriever when washed amnesiac down an obscure river to a new shore. It had seemed a sudden relief to shed the past, to feel free of lovers, husbands, and the stars which directed her destiny, to watch the huge and sudden gap between herself and the people who had wrenched her insides, to be distant for a short space.

All this made sense to us. It was superficially illogical, but it had an inner emotional logic beyond which questions became transgressions. The episode fitted no formula, its causes were hap-pily unknown and beyond the tax of ascertainment. Liz Taylor had come to us because she wanted a break, because she felt some unknown pull in our direction, and because we possessed that silent state of mind by which hospitality, being unspoken, is doubly communicated. We knew her visit would last only as long as the electric current which all three of us had generated held us together, that power breakdowns were inevitable, and that she would, like every wayfarer who makes a sojourn, soon enter that undiscovered country from whose bourne no traveller returns.

A few days went happily by and we showed her all the famous historic sights, the fading palaces, the arenas of war, the residences of conquerors, the tombs where flowers disguised the conquests of death.

'Gee honey,' said Liz by way of admiration after each monument, 'that looks kinda neat.'

But she seemed in search of something else for the old restive feeling came crowding back in her, and the sound of the 'Emperor' Concerto which caused the sun to rise each morning troubled in her an old vision, stirring within her the sight of a solitary grave in which a tree rose out of the earth in the shape of an upturned woman. With the ebb of fatigue her vision improved and she described it to us with greater clarity. 'Have either of you ever seen anything like that?' she asked. 'I'm trying to figure out what pulled me here.'

We were puzzling over this when my brother said again, in that way he always did. 'Hey man, put on the "Emperor" Concerto.'

'Okay,' I said. I opened our record box and put Beethoven's concerto on the slim, taut shaft of our record-changer, watching as it edged the record towards the inevitable orgasm. It was at that very moment, with the opening crash of an allegro, that we linked Liz's vision to what was commonplace in our lives, and which connected her with an unforeseen symmetry to people so distant from her world. We had seen precisely what she described. Suddenly that instant, switching on the 'Emperor', we knew it had switched on in Elizabeth's mind the exact location of suicidal despair, which we saw every day on our way to school.

We knew it all our lives as the grave of an unknown woman who died mysteriously during the Mutiny of 1857, leaving only a note that her remains be spared a churchyard, and that a single tree be planted by her side as protection. The tree that emerged had a double trunk which, at the appropriate height, overlapped and gave out the appearance of a woman's thighs. That grave, that tree, were almost the epicentre of our lives, lying halfway in our history, equidistant between the unspoken warmth of our mother's knitting needles and the dictations in reason we received at our school. They were for us a sight both beautiful and moving, connected through the current of our emotions and associations with the 'Emperor' Concerto, suddenly confirmed now by the vision which linked us to Liz.

I think it may have been at this point that some suspicion of the name of the woman in that grave began to grow within us, making us wonder at the strange contours of an emotional convergence between our world and the one from which Liz had arrived.

No official history of the Indian Mutiny of 1857 records the story of an English woman who, during the siege of the Residency, gave solace to the ears of the besieged with the only piano left in our town. Her music was not of sufficient consequence for history, the sound of her instrument drowned out by cannon and musket, by the crowds which closed in upon the precincts, leaving no room for softness or melody, leaving room only for the suicidal despair in which the woman wrote her note, asking only solitude, silence and space in the hereafter.

There was little left for us to do now, except get confirmation of what we suspected. We summoned the skeleton again and were pulled by him towards the grave where our unknown woman rested in peace, guarded by a solitary tree which grew with silent grace along the lines of her body.

Elizabeth paid him for the long haul and he left our world grinning. Elizabeth scraped the moss that obscured an epitaph.

We were right, of course, and as Elizabeth Taylor vanished from our sight we read what we had recently guessed but never bothered before to notice.

HERE LIES ELIZA TAYLOR
1827–1857
WHO WITH MELODY AND MUSIC LIT . . .

The gravestone broke off at that point, leaving us in the dark with further obvious questions – Who? How? What? Where? When? and Why?

Now, looking back, I attribute our feeling for the 'Emperor' Concerto and that singular perception of Elizabeth Taylor to an uncommon Anglicization which sensitized us to the beauties of the West, until the clamour of local historians sternly warned us against being so ideologically evil as to desire white before brown. Did Elizabeth Taylor grow in our minds and come electrically alive to compensate for the loss of her who so suffered from the Othello complex? Or did she spring to mind like a slow tree from the dust of a dead pianist who only desired solitude and music, as my brother would in the years to come? I cannot tell, though in later years we went native and adored the acceptably off-white actress Shabana Azmi to atone for our misguided youth, by which time the nationalist noise had given way to the feminist, dampening our desire altogether with Wills Filter evidence on the wicked lashings of power within all male sexuality.

But in those days of adolescent dreams, when we had the power to make the images of our minds come alive almost at will, the shadows of doubt cast upon us by that grave would very likely have taken up the rest of our short lives to pose and answer all those profound and overwhelming questions about the visionary and the real. We could have asked those questions endlessly, then posed them again and answered them a different way: they would have yielded no satisfactory answers. That was not a time for answers. To be alive then was to revel in the illogic of our minds and feelings, to witness the inner struggle of death and desire, to dream of Elizabeth Taylor and bring her home to bed on a rickshaw lit by an amnesiac satellite, to listen to Beethoven and connect his music with the image of a tree or the silent beauty of a grave. The happiness of our youth was no different from the ease with which our wildest dreams and desires came so intensely alive, assuming shapes with a furious, unpredictable anarchy. I remember now those wild and speculative days, when our images of passion culminated in that brief fusion of tempestuous impulse and suicidal despair which gave us, so strangely and unaccountably, the company of Elizabeth Taylor and the 'Emperor' Concerto.

5

The Secret Life of Mikhail Gorbachev

When my brother, who looked like Zeus, had his third emotional crisis, I saw the pattern in his life and rang up Gorbachev. Raisa picked up and said Gorby was on the pot, struggling with a recalcitrant flush-chain. 'They don't make them like they used to any more,' she said. 'It's all rusted up and clogged and nothing's going out.'

'Oh,' I said, thinking of my brother.

'I've phoned the German Chancellor,' she said. 'He's sending a plumber and a single-lever mixer. Isn't it exciting?'

'Yes,' I said. 'Very.'

My mind was on my brother. He had thick eyebrows and a handsome, hooded look. Once, when we were growing up together on the vulnerable Achilles, he told me, looking at a map in our Homer, that Sparta was located in a province called Laconia. Those names and the words that sprang out of them stuck in my mind, and an image of my brother, Spartan and silent, took root inside me, being modified only a little as the years passed.

'How're you, Doc? Is it urgent?' Raisa asked, returning to me. 'Shall I call Gorby out?'

I debated for five seconds and thought I'd try pulling the flush on my brother by myself. He needed badly to be dowsed in water to clear his head and feel undrowned by his third emotional crisis.

'No it's OK,' I said to Raisa. 'I'll call again if I need old Gorby's powerful mind.'

Raisa laughed affectionately. 'Yes,' she said. 'It was OK while he was into crumbling walls but he better get our flush in order or I'll crumble him.'

She sounded affectionate, and was, but I couldn't get away from feeling the low current of power and threat that often flowed just beneath so many of the things she said. I recalled the Raisa and Gorby I had known in New Delhi all those years ago, within the walls of the Lodi Gardens, by the flower-beds where they first met each other, and saw it was still the same between them. She was never in awe of him, not when they began, not now after he'd been king of all Europe. That felt nice. It made me feel people didn't fundamentally change with power, that relationships might, occasionally and unaccountably, transcend politics, that at least Gorby and she had managed to keep his politics out of their personal lives. I wondered if her mind, like Gorby's or mine, forged mysterious links between the old and ruined walls in Delhi by which we once walked and which never sealed their dead kings against the common touch, with others more unyielding, in Berlin and Moscow, that her husband had helped to crumble.

I thought then of my brother, who resembled Zeus, suffering his third emotional crisis, and the implications of the pattern in his life for all the people who cared for him.

'Our first single-lever mixer,' said Raisa.

She was often generous and concerned, but her own interests came first. An old feeling about her, a kind of emotional knowledge long lost, floated back inside me, reminding me that her personal excitements always swamped other considerations.

'What?' I asked, having briefly forgotten her single-lever mixer.

'You better come over and see all the new stuff Gorby and I are getting in from Europe, Doc.'

'Yes, yes,' I said. 'But I'm really ringing about my brother.'

'What?' she asked, focusing on to me again. 'You mean Jehova? What's up Doc?'

I knew Raisa would perk up and focus when I mentioned my brother. She lived a full life and was slow at focusing on things that didn't directly connect with her immediate needs. But affection lay dormant inside her. And besides, she was my brother's first emotional crisis and only collared Gorby on the rebound while he was licking her wounds. She always called my brother Jehova because he fitted better with her own image of outward sternness, which was just a veneer.

My brother only looked full of foreboding. It brought the women towards him in flocks. Inside he was silent and soft, and he suffered from short spells of intense sentimentality. Whenever he felt his life lacked grandeur, which was frequently, he worked himself up into a state of acute morbidness by reading *Hamlet*. That made him feel depressed and grand. He wallowed and revelled in tragedy. Outwardly he was always calm and taught history with the correct degree of passion, though he said his discipline was only a jumble of contending perspectives and had nothing to do with the truth. From our early years we'd both got accustomed to believing in fiction. Once, when Raisa asked my brother what he was made of, he said formally, as though he'd thought it through carefully, that his insides consisted entirely of milk, water and gelatine. 'When you move me,' he said with his hilarious solemnity, 'the jelly quivers and makes me emotional.'

'The usual thing,' I said to Raisa. 'Just another woman he's got hooked up with and doesn't know how to disconnect. He says it'll pass.'

'Oh hell, not again,' said Raisa. 'How old is Jehova now? Stop pulling that blessed chain for a minute Gorbs,' she yelled.

Even her brief distraction on the line gave me a little time to myself, and I felt distant from the telephone, from her voice, from the universe. I took myself off to a satellite in the sky that made slow, Sisyphean circles round the world. I was its lonely, spaced-out occupant. I wore a tracksuit and jogged in circles inside my satellite. A Golden Retriever trotted at my heels and in the empty space forever ahead Beethoven played the 'Appassionata' with his fingertips and his hair. I felt free of people. An amnesiac moon on its own circular trip showed me the Great Wall of China, reminding me of Elizabeth Taylor and our vulnerable Achilles. But this wall stood firm. It didn't look vulnerable. It didn't look as though Gorby or anyone else was about to make it hit the sack.

'Jehova?' I asked Raisa feebly.

I felt and sounded absent-minded on the phone line. There was an international resonance on account of my voice having to travel to Raisa by satellite. It delayed my voice and gave it an echo that made me feel hollow. In my mind I had moved on to Alexandria, where the early church fathers developed out of Jehova. An early father there, Origen, though inclined in his philosophy towards the sublime, castrated himself to staunch the flow of passion. I saw him climb a Platonic ladder to a barsati* from where he saw the rainy Pleiades vex a dim sea, shining out without ambiguity in the night sky.

'What's up with you and Jehova, Doc?' I heard Raisa ask. 'You know I mean *my* Jehova, don't you? He was the first one for me, Doc. First one is the worst,' she added with what I recalled as her rare, caring Russian laugh. 'It's kind of difficult to get the first one out of your system, Doc, specially if he's choked you up with love for years like God. Maybe that's why our flush systems are all clogged,' she added, chuckling impulsively with the thought.

I was getting impatient. The phone corporation was drilling a hole through my pocket and she was still trying out tentative conversational profundities.

'Is it bad again?' she asked more urgently, perhaps sensing the impatience in my silence. My brother was the first one in her bloodstream and her residual feeling for him was a certain indication she still hadn't quite been able to flush him out of her system.

'Well he's now in his thirties,' I said, 'and says it'll pass. But it doesn't look that great to me.'

'Oh hell,' she said, confirming what I felt. 'Who's the girl? Never mind. Hey Gorbs,' she yelled in Russian, and came back to

* Delhi Hindi for 'rooftop flat'.

me. 'I better tell Gorbs to meet Jehova soon,' she said. 'He's great at pulling people out of these stupid messes. Hang on a minute. I'm sure he'll love going back to Delhi to see you both.'

I hung on for a minute and visualized her going off to tell Gorby about my brother, her first lover, and thought of her days with my Greek-god brother, who she called Jehova, and of how he slowly fell out of love with her while she clung to him, a remote and adjudicating deity.

Mikhail Gorbachev chanced upon her in the Lodi Gardens one winter day. She was sitting under a tenebrous tree, smoking a Marlboro Mild. He was out for a walk with his two pet monkeys, Lenin and Trotsky, one on each shoulder. He'd trained them to put lice into his thinning hair. He would make them leave the lice to wander off and hide in his scalp, after which the monkeys would pick them out and eat them up, their hands moving from scalp to mouth with an urgent indifference. His strong sense of the bizarre made him irreverent and very good at rescuing lost souls. It seemed consistent with his own sense of the absurd that he, a man born never to rule, should have been driven by Raisa, once she'd acquired him in the Lodi Gardens, to assume in their later years an authority that he only wanted everyone to flout. By temperament he was a breaker of rules and she their maker.

He saw her in the shadow of the dead kings that lay in the Lodi Gardens and knew she was a lost soul, suffering cosmic gloom on a park bench. She told me later, sitting on my brother's lap in his Defence Colony barsati, that Gorby looked a three-headed Hanuman, appearing like that with Lenin and Trotsky. It was her farewell session with my brother: there was only affection between them once she knew she'd got Gorby on her leash. The monkey god saved her from Jehova and she carried him off to make him King of Russia. She was much more into power than he ever was, and she settled for what seemed a regal possibility when she found her deity, my brother, shaking free. I was glad for my brother, and he was too, for himself and for me. Raisa could be wrathful, like Kali. She mostly got what she wanted to get, and, after the initial surge of blinding emotion had passed, my brother was afraid she wanted him.

Of course all this was a long time ago in a garden where the dead were nicely hidden by domes and flowers, and to be fair to her she didn't know then that she and Gorby would become king and queen. I sensed her motivations, the subdued affection and the impulse, but can't say I really knew what stirred her jelly. Like everyone, she had a complicated inside. She genuinely cared for people she could mould. The small circle of dystopian aesthetes in which I moved with my brother was more sure about her than I was. They knew she had Europe in her bones, and that Gorby was doomed to get her all she wanted. After she stopped wanting my brother and had run through Gorby, she wanted Europe. There was no way, then, that he was going to carry on wandering the Delhi parks, with Lenin and Trotsky on his shoulders, for to get her Europe he had to get a move on in life and be King of Russia. His nomadic life was done when Raisa decided on him. Our small circle foresaw him being somewhat smothered by her, but we had Europe in our bones too and were not unsympathetic to Raisa. Something of her was in all of us. We lusted madly after Europe, where the streets were often free of people, sipping Old Monk in our barsatis at the margins of our city, falling in love now and again with each other and feeling depressed by the shortage of space around our lives.

That was many years ago, before things really began to crumble, inside people and all around them.

Raisa was back on the line. 'If it's serious Gorby'll fly over to Delhi tomorrow,' she said.

'Thanks,' I said. It was nice to know he hadn't changed with power. I recalled his Forsterian heart; if he had to choose between saving his country and saving his friend, he wouldn't think twice. In his personal life, which came first, he behaved as though the soul of a man he knew came before the soul of the country where he had been king. His politics seemed to flow out of that quiet vaguely Nehruvian sort of vision.

'How're Lenin and Trotsky?' I asked Raisa. 'Can Gorby bring them along?'

Gorby's magic with people always worked better when the monkeys were with him, as it had with Raisa all those years ago in the Lodi Gardens. It was as though his deeply emotional ability to communicate depended in some obscure way upon the weight of the two monkeys on his shoulders.

'Yes,' she said, 'they're older and not so playful now but they're still clinging to him. I'll tell him to take them along. I don't really get along with them on their own anyway. Remember to carry peanuts and bananas to the airport, Doc, or they'll drive you nuts,' she said, chuckling again, this time invitingly, at her small joke. She was always fishing for admiration, but I wasn't in a very obliging mood.

'Yes OK,' I said tonelessly, then felt a flash of guilt. 'How's Wanda?' I asked by way of compensation.

That was the name of her new goldfish and I knew she felt personally wanted if people asked after its general health. It seemed in character for her to offset Lenin and Trotsky with Wanda. Gorby couldn't feel for fish and so had merely an aesthetic interest in them, but I thought he probably approved of Wanda as a concept. I had realized soon after I got to know him that, in fact, like Polanski, he didn't merely approve of the irreverent and the bizarre but was frequently moved by it. The idea of a fish called Wanda in such tranquil and domestic proximity with Lenin and Trotsky seemed a notion in harmony with his general way of thinking. It was also in keeping with their relationship, their way of undercutting each other while staying close. Raisa got a real kick out of gazing for hours at something that didn't drown in water. It made her nicely different from Gorby, who saw sense in monkeys, dogs and horses, none in frogs and fish.

But my mind was on my brother. He was different from them both. My brother's mind was flooded with drowned sailors.

I tried a mind-over-matter job with my bladder, clogging up my pipe by shifting in spasms from one leg to another, while Raisa told me about the particular yellowness of her goldfish. I imagined prizing open Wanda's mouth, unzipping, easing myself carefully in, feeling the relief as the yellowness left me and bloated Wanda, watching the fish balloon from gold to jaundice yellow before exploding into crumbs that looked like bits of the Berlin Wall.

'Can you hear me?' Raisa asked urgently from Russia.

'Yes, that's wonderful,' I said, clutching my crotch and shifting weight. She'd been going on about the virtues of the new fishfood she'd got from Elizabeth Taylor.

'I've heard about Horizon Fishcrumbs too,' I said. 'It's drowning out our TV with its ads about having all the hormones that open up gills and let the fish breathe easily.'

'Yes, Doc,' she said. 'Cuts out the aquamarine claustrophobia, they say.'

That sounded too nice a phrase to have been spontaneous. She must have got it from some ad I'd missed. She really hadn't changed at all, I thought. There seemed still the same interest in variety and new words. I flashed to a scene from an old film we once saw together, in which Dirk Bogarde asked his secretary if she approved of violence. 'No,' said the secretary. 'Neither do I,' said Bogarde. 'It reeks of spontaneity.'

'Shall I send you a packet of Horizon Fishcrumbs through Gorbs?' Raisa asked considerately.

'I don't have a fish,' I said, 'and I've got to piss.'

'What?' she asked with some incredulity. She probably thought she misheard me. Doubts were too minor to clog her mind, and she just went on in her mildly frenetic way. 'Then get one, Doc,' she said. 'They're very soothing. Why don't you get one for Jehova? Get him a, what's it called, pomfret? It'll soothe him down and if he doesn't like watching it swim he can eat it.'

She was distracted and unfocused again. Her immediate concerns were switching her off the inner life even now. Still, I was glad her years with Gorby had infected her with his affection for the grotesque. I was also very full of fluid and she wasn't letting

91

me off the hook. She was bad at that. If she felt someone going without feeling she was letting them go, she felt they'd beaten her. I suppose some people feel like that on account of their mothers having taken away the nipples too early from their mouths. It was the opposite with my brother, though, and helped him become a homoeopathic gynaecologist and gave him that suckling tenderness with womankind.

'Come Mr Talleyrand, tally me banana.' Belafonte had arrived in my stereo. I twiddled his knob and he piped down. His sentence circled in my mind and summoned up Gorby's arrival in Delhi, with Lenin and Trotsky eating bananas and lice off his shoulders. I sucked in my stomach and pressed my crotch. There was a mirror by the phone. I looked past it to a door that gave to an empty pot. I knew if I pulled the chain above it the waters would gush out obligingly, cleaning out all the yellowness I might put in. I remembered Gorby saying, once, that life's most overrated pleasure was a good screw, its most underrated a good shit. My brother's life looked immersed in it, and it required a fine flushing system inside his bloodstream to stop him clogging. Gorby, I knew, was more than a passable plumber.

'I'll pick Gorby up from the airport tomorrow,' I said to Raisa. 'Tell him to look out for the bearded guy with the banana in his hands.'

She laughed at that. 'You don't have to do that, Doc,' she said. 'He'll probably pick you out from the airplane.'

We made pecking noises on the phone by way of fond farewells. Two parrots in an anaesthetist's cage had made similar sounds during Nehru's lifetime and in the year he died, and the perfect logic of my mind caused me to recall Mark Antony and Octavius Caesar gasping for breath over Elizabeth Taylor.

Below my brother's barsati the daily queues of women were forming. When he was not a historian, my brother was a homoeopathic gynaecologist. He was greatly into healing biodegradable women non-invasively. In my mind I saw the forms of other queues near Raisa's house, blanched and snaking slowly towards Lenin's tomb, of couples newly married. They looked happy in the cold, awaiting patiently the impending benediction from the tomb of a king whose bones were fast crumbling. I saw in my mind a half skeleton grinning liplessly at the women in white, carrying flowers. His sockets gazed blindly at pearls that were once his eyes, now on the necks of women in white. My brother didn't look anything like that, of course. He was handsome and tall and wholesome and strong, and tender with the women who waited in queues to be seen by him.

Sometimes there were only Rajasthani women, many in vermilion, with the thirst of the deserted around their eyes. A cluster of them once sat gracefully by the side-lane below the barsati, scattering their red smocks around them, looking like upturned poppies. I imagined the sibilant hiss of piss that only comes out of women. It gave me a momentary flutter of joy and stirred the little one sleeping in my crotch. I shifted weight in the correct way and he went back to sleep. The women rose gracefully, stepping aside from their little puddles. The queue moved forward slowly, half a shuffle at a time. A gold-brown dog with furrowed eyes sat close by, her legs crossed over with a protective daintiness. She seemed to watch the ritual unmovingly.

Once I asked one of the women in the queue, who was a regular, what she got out of seeing my brother. I never asked my brother how he went about healing the women who queued up for him, or what exactly homoeopathic gynaecology involved. It always sounded to me like a sort of euphemism for something better, not a profession. But I kept my wickeder thoughts to myself, for though we were brothers we liked savouring the deliciousness of the unsaid. It would have broken a low wall between us that we both cherished if I'd asked him a personal question. I didn't need to anyway. But it felt nice to ask a woman who queued up for him what it was all about. I could tell just by looking at her that she'd suffered through English Honours at some posh college and taken to men. I thought she might have lots of literary lines stuffed inside her jelly, but she was simpler.

'It's because we're all pretty fucked up,' I suppose, she said, 'except when we're with someone special like him. It's a kind of fix. Very healing. Doesn't everyone need a fix? What's yours?'

She was into American quickness and repartee, and I wasn't sure I wanted further elucidation about her life, or about my brother's as a homoeopathic gynaecologist. I remembered instead the slow movement of the 'Emperor' Concerto and the gentle eyes of elephants, and retreated.

It sounded pretentious to reply 'Beethoven'.

'Music,' I said.

My brother's second emotional crisis was the least serious. Her breasts were as shapely as the Spiral Nebulae but she was like clingfilm, and at first my brother didn't realize he was only lusting after her. All the usual tenderness had welled up in him and blinded him to the truth that beneath it all he didn't care a fuck about her. Later he felt very guilty about it all. It made him introspective for a few days and got him hooked on Thomas Hardy for a short while, till his emotional need for wallowing in the tragic destinies of beautiful women greatly wronged had been satisfied. But he always knew women would smother him and that the second one was no better in that respect. He felt guilty about her, as he did about his indifference for our mother, but he disentangled himself gently, trying all the time not to hurt her.

After that, until his third crisis, my brother ran through the daily queues of women that were constituted for him with the silence of a knife. The women stepped down from his Defence Colony barsati one at a time, some slowly, others quickly on account of departing buses, flicking their sarees to get in one final touch of order, looking contented, sometimes checking the colour of their hairlines, the vermilion scattered around them.

My brother's third emotional crisis slowed him down. It made him look and feel older, his face looked heavier in the mirror. I would have said 'fuller' were I not so vicariously narcissistic, always imagining myself as him and feeling inhibited about admitting the truth. I felt helpless, as on the earlier two occasions, because I couldn't get personal with my godlike brother or ask him about the latest girl. It would pass, but he needed flushing out then, to make it pass. I phoned Gorby and Raisa because they were distant, powerful, and cared about him. He looked like Zeus and later Beethoven and was made of some special jelly which must have gone into him on account of our mother always letting herself into his mouth and denying me. Later, when she died slowly, he behaved like the dispassionate historian he never was. I did the nursing and felt drained.

I met Gorbachev, Lenin and Trotsky off the Aeroflot flight. Lenin grabbed the bananas, Trotsky took the peanuts. Gorby had a sack slung over his shoulder. We got in the car after bear hugs. 'You look Bushed,' I said, having rehearsed the joke several times over since the phone call. We held hands in the car. We were old comrades and went back a long time, since our days together in the Lodi Gardens, where the dead kings stored their bones, from before the time he saved Jehova from Kali, looking a triadic Hanuman and getting collared into being King of Russia by a woman on a park bench smoking a Marlboro Mild.

'What's in the sack?' I asked.

'I call it my Cul-de-Sac,' he said, laughing hugely and drawing me in.

He was like that, very infectious. He could crumble things or mend them, or do it the other way round, just as he liked. I never saw anyone as good as Gorby with people. Being with him was like being with my brother.

'It's got bits of the Berlin Wall in it,' he said. 'Want a piece? It's sort of symbolic of the times, Doc. Keep a bit. I've been handing it out to anyone who wants a souvenir.'

'OK,' I said, and dipped into the sack. Lenin and Trotsky were looking at me. They were trained to observe the ritual.

'What's up with Jehova?' Gorby asked.

Our hands were firmly cemented with a fast balm which thence did spring. The waters flew out from under the head of a virgin, raped and dead and wearing white, in a Bergman movie. There's only truth in fiction, I thought. I thought of my brother, who looked like Zeus but was vulnerable like Achilles, and of Gorby's days with Raisa that had made him succumb to thinking of my brother as a lesser deity.

'It's his third crisis and he's getting old,' I said. 'He needs some of your healing touch and your monkey tricks.'

My brother and I and Gorbachev felt like the eternal triangle, sitting together in the Defence Colony barsati. My brother was silent early in the evening. The evil hormones had been flooding his bones. He was thinking about Phlebas the drowned Phoenician and the undersea currents picking his bones in whispers. There were lots of stray literary lines mixed up with the jelly inside him. I was thinking about Elizabeth Taylor playing the part of a hypotenuse. Lenin and Trotsky were doing their tricks and going at the Old Monk. Belafonte was singing the Jamaica Farewell in the stereo. 'Rum is fine any time ayear.'

Gorby knew when to relax and when to talk. He sat with us in that small room in a warm and peaceful silence. For all his liveliness and levity, he possessed the gift of silence. Quietness never embarrassed him. He could be strong and silent or weak and voluble, as the occasion required. That evening he let Lenin and Trotsky get sozzled on the Old Monk and slowly nursed his own Bloody Mary. Though he'd taught them their tricks, he shared our mirth. Lenin dressed up as Al Capone, smoked a cigar and quoted from Kissinger's Memoirs. Trotsky did a difficult Reagan imitation: he had to sit still for a whole minute, looking dumb and grinning sheepishly from ear to ear.

I could never tell Lenin from Trotsky. The years and continuous proximity had made them look even more like each other than they once did, as happens to husbands and wives who start off looking only like themselves and end up looking like brother and sister. But my brother, who knew history and was passionate about animals, could always distinguish Lenin from Trotsky. He tickled their chins and chattered away with them in different directions that led nowhere.

I disappeared for a space into Dostoevsky, to where Ivan Karamazov saw Turkish soldiers throw infants into the air, catching them on bayonets as they fell. Later, when Lenin and Trotsky had passed into a stupefied sleep, cuddled up with my brother under his blankets, Gorby and I talked about many things, about Raisa's latest passion for fish and the latest in sanitaryware. The Russian cold still froze the taps and he said it was a good thing she was badgering the German Chancellor for new pipes that never clogged. We recalled the ruin of kings and the beds of flowers along the walls where we had walked, and of the many things that would not yield. Like Nehru, he made politics sound as though it had something to do with human beings.

On the main road in the distance a traffic jam was building up. Through the distant horns of motorcars Gorby worked the Hippocratic oath. I twiddled the TV to check on the daily cabinet reshuffle, then realized Gorby needed a holiday from all quests for power. I electrocuted the latest cabinet by twiddling another knob and saw, in the shade of the television's goodbye flash, an instant of pleasure on Gorby's tired face.

'It's so democratic to finish with politics like that,' he said.

I saw the emotional fatigue, the toll of falling walls. He needed a break just as much as my brother, and I was glad Raisa and I had haphazardly, through our telephone talk, organized one for them together.

I rang Raisa the next morning to tell her Gorby'd arrived safely and that things seemed OK for my brother with him around. But she wasn't about to give me a chance to start.

'Chancellor Kohl's sent the single-lever mixer and the plumber's fixed it up,' she said. 'It feels just like Europe. Come over, Doc.

Give Gorby the phone. Tell him to bring Jehova and you back on the return flight. You've got to see this tap flow.'

'OK OK,' I said, feeling something start up inside me. Maybe nipple-denial got me so my kidneys get going just when someone's on the line. I looked at the mirror near the phone and saw in it the image of my brother.

'Gorby's just taken Jehova off to the hills for a few days,' I said. 'The change should do him good.'

'Great,' she said. 'I'm glad they've gone into the country. Gorby needs the change too, Doc. He needs to get way from all these city walls. How's he doing, Doc?' she wanted to know.

'Fine,' I said. 'They'll both be fine, I think.'

They both needed more space and clean air to flush out the pollution, I thought, and Raisa seemed to think so too. I wondered if Raisa had ever felt anything else for me on the occasions we'd been together all those years ago, during moments when our feelings and thoughts had seemed to coincide. But she was with my brother then, and later with Gorby, and my stray thought soon faded out like the slow dissipation of an image in an old movie, leading to other images, another story.

I thought instead of the Phoenician sailor, of the aesthetic satisfaction in my bowels after a morning clearance, of the absence of traffic on a broad road, of Dick Francis trampled untimely on a race track, of Beethoven's wild-calm eyes and the slow movement of elephants, and of the composure in my jaw muscles after listening to the 'Emperor' Concerto.

'How's your flush system doing?' I asked Raisa.

But our connection failed just at that moment, and, though I strained my ears to keep our link, I only managed to hear Raisa's reply being drowned by the unchained roar of cascading water. I apprehended another flood in my life, something that would arrive punctually like a cow or an identity crisis to give further shape to my brother's life and mine.

Patiently, like an old man in a dry season, I waited for rain.

6

S/he, or *A Postmodern Chapter on Gender and Identity**

It was late in the evening and the July clouds were coming in low outside, swift and slowing grey. I saw them gather to a dark intensity from my office and soon a drizzle began to slant against the window-panes, settling on everything with a fine sense of equality. I watched the drizzle slate into a fierce rain which tried hard to break through. It stopped to a drumroll against impenetrable glass but the atmosphere behind ate its way in and went straight for my body, searching like the devil for my soul. I looked at my watch. It was nearly time to leave. I was expected at a party.

But the world outside was a sea. I stood helpless in my office and saw a road below heave to the torrent, then swell to an ocean. I felt myself grow old surrounded there in my office, compelled by the rain and the mood under my skin and one stray weather-beaten memory. As the black tar of that Delhi road dissolved into an opaque grey film, I saw myself shade into a Hemingway hero. I was keen on literary characters and sometimes, when the prospects were bleak and the weather seemed to insinuate its way into my epidermis, I imagined myself as some loner or the other. And so, that evening, a solitary witness to the savagery of rain, I felt myself become the old man and the sea below was my world.

The old man rigged out his skiff and set sail with his tackle. He

* 'S/he' is hereafter spelt 'she' on account of what my brother says is called 'the ocular imperative', i.e. the need for words to look right on the page. Therefore, this chapter is dedicated to the memory of H. Rider Haggard.

was in a small boat and looked fragile in it. He looked at his brown hands, the hair on edge over his arms and the palms of his hands wrecked with lines. Two minutes into the deep and he was surrounded by sharks.

'Pancho,' said the old man absently, 'O Pancho . . .' the rest of his sentence beaten by the cosmos. He paused for breath and surveyed the elements, the big fish and his little catamaran. He saw the thrash of a multitudinous sea incarnadined and the tails which slashed the sky like windscreen wipers. They were ranged against him in vast circles of rubber which spilled over the horizon. He was overcome by the feeling that this was not his world, that this was a world he did not know. He felt the weather seep into his guts and a vicious sky fall upon him, he saw the merciless ocean surround him and knew there was nothing to do except try and survive. The old man threw out a line.

Before he knew it he had been hooked by a shark.

From my office window I watched the old man struggle against the big dark shark. The rhythm of the rain on his arms and the sweat on his brow and the salt of the sea felt like flecks eroding his frail body as he tried to reel in that shark. He remembered what his father had told him about the Delhi shark as he pulled at the end of his tether and he tried hard, the old man, to forget what his father had told him those many years back when he was a boy: 'They get you in the end.'

This shark was strong. He was made in India and had ISI certification branded on his blubber. He had guts and movement, he had cut his teeth against a lot of old men and boats, his muscles honed by the sharp tang of the sea. The old man hadn't bargained for a shark with small eyes and stilettoes sticking out of his jaws so you could see all the way through his mouth to eternity.

'This is like Moby Dick,' said the old man through his teeth, 'or Hemingway on a bad day. How did I get into this soup?' And then his words were whisked to oblivion by a gust and he knew that he was all alone in a universe of fictions. 'Pancho,' said the old man. 'It's either you or me.'

The old man had a windscreen wiper in his hand which he used as a harpoon. It stung the fish no harder than his words. That shark was in business. First he turned into an albino whale, then he chewed up the bow, after that the stern, and finally all the elements that keep a character afloat. The old man was destined for the deep.

I watched myself go down with regret and wondered if one of the several narratives of death I forged in my imagination would ultimately prove a premonition. On gloomy days I had several going together: plunging into a sea of sharks was possible from an airplane struck by lightning or terrorists too, or just by driving on the road outside. Going under in the sea of Delhi seemed the strongest possibility.

But soon my reverie softened, then disappeared with the rain. The traffic unfrenzied and the last drops dripped down my office signboard. They glistened in the neon light which gave a little sheen to the See-Through Detective Agency where I plied my trade. Business had been bad all day. No harassed wives had called. Brides didn't burn on rainy afternoons. The men of Delhi saved their deconstruction for dry weather. The phone was in a coma. The police had cracked down on dowry.

I looked outside my office. The humidity was so thick you needed an umbrella just to keep the moisture out. On the road which spilled into my door the steam rose, hesitated awhile, lost its nerve, and was run over by traffic. It seemed okay to leave. I got in my car. My windscreen wipers slashed the sky.

Mostly I fight shy of large parties and loathe arriving late to one. The problem is existential: how to compose one's jaw muscles when walking the plank towards a thrashing sea. But I couldn't get off the hook on this party. I had to get there with four loaves of bread and five kilos of Perfect Ice to help work the miracle of engaging a multitude with false conversation. My brother, a struggling historian, was like a lakeside fisherman attracting shoals. He liked his infrequent barsati parties to click.

On such occasions I had to act the apostle, serve out wine like water, and crease a smile on my face for his guests.

Tyres whirled on the roads which led to my brother's barsati. Every man in Delhi bristled with hostility and drove as though his life depended on it. It took more than an hour of guerilla tactics to fight through dowry fiends to buy the food and ice, then a titanic struggle through an ocean of rubber to reach my brother's barsati.

When I reached the party there were twenty people already in. Walking cautiously through the door I heard snatches of their conversation.

'O hi Shamim my dear where have you been all summer my life's been bereft . . . O hi Ruksie baby I must say you're looking good have you been up in the high . . . O yes I want it stiff please no no no I say yes just a bit more take it easy aah shit it's fallen get a cloth . . . okay soda if there's . . . but have you heard Mukul's got the Commonwealth . . . just let that wine breathe there's only one . . . life . . .'

I worked up a genial expression and put purpose in my tread to make it seem I wasn't sidling in. It helped to be carrying something into the barsati. With the bread and ice for protection I felt armed.

The air was thick with cocktail colours and cries of welcome. People gushed and fell on each other with a monsoon enthusiasm. It was the usual crowd of academics bracing themselves for the new university term, plus a few journalists, a couple of cinema buffs, all struggling intellectuals who worked in archives and libraries, their lives ringed by peons, clerks, bureaucrats, politicians and all the other big fish of the city. I walked in to warm greetings and soon merged into a happy haze of friendly chatter. I was relieved by the speed with which one world dissolved and gave room to another. Beyond me I heard a familiar, reassuring babble:

'I don't know about life but there's money in Gender . . . so when's he leaving . . . not another job Shiraz leave something for your next life . . . but have you heard Lavatri Alltheorie's got a job in the Univ . . . Jesus it's a miracle . . . for Chrissake just let that wine breathe there's only one . . .'

Bits of all this talk registered, specially one bit: Alltheorie was coming to teach in India! Jesus! I'd heard my brother speak with great awe about that lady. She was the Moby Dick of the American academy who'd jumped out of the Indian Ocean to rule the Pacific and the Atlantic. He called her the Great Brown S/he. From what I had been able to make out, Alltheorie was the killer-diller of the new discipline called Gender Studies which had emerged out of the Women's Movement. I had some experience of some of the genuine people within it, having investigated cases for several of the women who helped rehabilitate harassed wives. Those women were straight. They spoke a language I followed. They weren't businesswomen.

Alltheorie was. She was located at the rarefied end of the Women's Movement where Lit.Crit. became Lit.Clit. She possessed a vocabulary to which my brother and his friends aspired. In their world there was a jargon phrase for her sort of fish. Post-modernist theoretician, boa deconstructor, discourse analyst, post-structuralist critic, feminist historian of subalternity, colonialism and gender. It was big business. I recalled what I had Scotch-taped into a mental picture of my brother's goddess. I did a swift vocabulary change to get into the right narrative mode: I couldn't exactly impale her in the language of my brother's crowd, but I did my best.

Professor Lavatri Alltheorie, once a medium-sized Bengali gent, was now a lady of very substantial proportions. As a diasporic Indian academic who taught packed courses on the Semiology of Deconstruction and the Deconstruction of Semiology to a white student audience, she had weighed nature against nurture and carefully considered the ontological implications of changing her sex before taking the plunge. Or as her seventh gay lover Professor Gyandeo Bhaiya-Sabko put it, before taking the plunger out. The difficulties she'd faced when making that decision were enormous. She (or rather he, which is what she was) realized as one grounded in the praxis of theory that the decision to deconstruct one's Self into the Other did not merely involve gender: it involved gender, race and class, Freud, Fanon and Foucault. It was difficult enough being brown in a white world. Being also a culturally underprivileged brown male in a blue-collar institution dominated by men with white masks, black thoughts and repressed neo-colonial urges was worse. And then to compound one's subalternity that one final step further by becoming a brown woman in a white upper-class male universe . . . even Professor Bhaiya-Sabko, acknowledged for his treatise on female strategies of everyday resistance, had suggested caution against such apocalyptic physiological de(con)struction. Unfortunately it was precisely the absences and silences within his arguments, which he imbricated in feudal, genuflective tropes such as pleading on bended knees, that had overdetermined his lover's need to counter patriarchy as symbolized by the oppressive institution of monogamous coupledom.

Baby take a load of that. And then some. They didn't speak straight in my brother's trade. In the waters at which he gazed with such longing it literally didn't pay to be understood. It paid to be Lavatri Alltheorie.

She was the Tiresias of Gender Studies. Like that noble hermaphrodite she'd seen both sides of the sex coin. Not that she was into small change. She'd raked in the notes in the deconstruction business. She decoded peasants, ladies, gents, you name it. Professor Alltheorie's *Collected Marxist Phonecalls* had outsold *Gone With the Wind*. The phone company which published that book made enough money to organize a coup in Chile; they made a killing with her tome. Her *Collected Feminist Faxes* was in press. Her opponents defined her subject-position with a law – Lavatri's Law: Incredible Articulation + Incredible Incomprehensibility = Incredible Salary. By rumour she paid alimony to seven husbands and palimony to their seven predecessors. Socially she had the reputation of charming the pants off any man.

In the distance behind everyone seemed agog with excitement

over Alltheorie's arrival from metropolis to periphery. I wondered why Professor Alltheorie was changing places, how she'd fare in our small world, where she'd lodge, who she'd board. But I kept a safe distance. I didn't know if there was some essential me, and if I did I wouldn't have confessed it to my brother or his friends, but I did know that I was comfortable with a different set of words. Once more an old feeling gnawed at me, the unease of an old man in an alien ocean. This was not my world and, as the 'Emperor' Concerto got switched on by an automatic hormone in my mind, I knew I belonged somewhere else, where ships had anchors and words a straighter meaning. Not that I was ever too sure where I belonged. I seemed in a perpetual state of identity crisis, swimming in a tidal wave of literary narratives, and outside my own mind, sometimes, everything took on the resonance of a turbulent sea. Not always, but enough to make me keep aloof.

Shamim had brought along her daughter. She was talking to a man I didn't know. Their conversation called me down from reverie and the satellites I saw zigzagging in the sky like traffic through an opaque sea of stars.

'Divya's only four years old and she says Oh hell, and I'm seven and a half and I don't even say Oh heaven.'

The stranger and I both laughed at that. It drew me into their chatter. I liked that little girl. I was glad she'd come to the party.

'And who is Divya?'

'She's my cousin. She's four years old but she's not in my school. She's only in the K.G.'B'. Can I have some beer?'

The stranger and I blinked and looked at our glasses.

'Shall we ask your mama?' he asked finally.

'I hope she's drunk,' said the little girl. 'If she's drunk she'll say yes.' She skipped off in Shamim's direction.

'Precocious little thing, isn't she?' he said.

'Sweet kid,' I said, and gave him my name.

'Pankaj Chopra,' he replied, 'Pancho for short.' He winked and smiled wickedly but he looked warm and full of fun. Not something with bite. I was pleasantly surprised. He didn't seem part of the intelligentsia on my brother's barsati. He seemed my sort. With him and the kid there I felt relaxed.

'So where d'you teach?' I ventured.

'Teach? That's about as far as you can be from where I am. Teachers scare the wits out of me. Specially social science. I'm a doc. Live in the US of A. Hawaii to be precise. I'm Mukul's cousin. Staying with him, so he brought me along. How 'bout yourself?'

'Detective agency,' I said. 'Private eye. I specialize in matrimonial cases.'

'That's very appropriate,' he said with a laugh. 'Private eye sounds about right for marital affairs. You'll do better if you pry harder, hah hah hah. Come to think of it I'm more or less in the same business myself. I started off as a kidney and gall-bladder specialist. Good business till I got technologically obsolete. After that I moved into hi-tech. Erection machines. Then that went limp. Now I'm in the gender business. I deconstruct. I do sex-change, hah hah hah.'

I was amused; also pleasantly mystified. My detection antenna went on the hop.

Shamim's little girl had a Campa Cola in her hands. In the next room the couples began a clutch-and-shuffle. A cassette was switched to Jethro Tull. The couples went into a frenzy.

'How d'you mean technologically obsolete?'

'Ah that. O well I guess that's always happening. In your biz for instance, if someone invented a periscope that worked via satellite and could be hooked into a TV monitor through a dish antenna, I guess you'd be out of business pretty damn quick too. Wives would be lying next to their lovers and tracking husbands while looking at a screen. You'd be technologically obsolescent.'

I looked at the sky in alarm. The Milky Way had curdled with satellites. I unrolled the bottoms of my trousers.

'It was the medical equivalent of that sort of peephole that did me in. I was happily operating, left, right and centre, frontways and sideways, for gall stones, kidney stones, gall stones, kidney stones. There were miles of stones to go before I slept. And you can say that again. The money was coming in hand over fist.'

He paused, and his cigarette glowed to a reflective pull.

'The world was full of stones and I was happy. And then the bloody Germans came in with their stone crusher. The Adolf Lithotripter it was called. I had to check out lithotripter in my dic. Stone breaker, it said. A great gadget. No operations. You just had to duck the patient in a tub of water and bombard her frontals with ultrasound rays. The stones got dissolved non-invasively. Just like that. End of story. End of bloody business for me. I had to rush around like a headless chicken the next couple of years trying to find people with stones who hadn't got to that godawful stone crusher. But you know what the Germans are like. Efficient. They mounted a great advertising campaign. They sold their Adolf 'Tripter in every one-horse town in the US of A. They sublicensed their patent, they lowered their price, they did me in. They crushed me with that gadget. It was too large for a solo operator. But it got into every hospital. I got squashed. I went out of business.'

'You don't look too squashed,' I said with a laugh.

A storyteller, I thought, as I felt my vocabulary move to the world of John Wayne and Humphrey Bogart to accommodate Pancho within the correct narrative framework. My brother and his friends would have called Pancho different. Master Narrator. Or Metropolitan Discursive Informant maybe. Yeah. They had a different feel for words, my brother's crew. Yeah. Sure thing. Mentally, I chewed a cigar and narrowed my eyes, then nonchalantly spat. I flung five aspirin tablets in the air and sprayed them out into a cloud with my six-shooter. Then I shifted identities and got back to being my essentialist me.

I was glad Pancho had blundered into that party. It was the first party in which I felt unfratricidal. It seldom happens that way, but it does just when you're expecting different. My moods were as unpredictable as my narrative modes and about as uncertain as the next world; I kept them safely distant from my inviolate self and stayed faithful to one. Equanimity. Happiness was a transient phenomenon, like cash in my current account. I didn't bank on it. If it came in with the weather, great. Most days it came in with the booze. Each day's accumulated depression dissolved in the evening's lake of liquor. Two stiff drinks sloshing in the guts and my jaw muscles settled into all the composure of an afterlife. It stopped me wondering who I was. I was Wayne. I was Bogart. I was Melville and Hemingway. I was Paul Newman and Paul deMan. Once in a way Nehru. Roll over Beethoven. I was Whitman. I encompassed multitudes.

Soon I felt another vocabulary change come over me and I began to think in the words of Pancho's world. On my brother's barsati, where I was accustomed to flounder among the seaweeds of deconstruction, that was an unusual feeling.

Pancho had resumed his compelling narrative.

'Squashed? I wasn't squashed, I was dissolved, bankrupt, broken, kaput. The Huns got me by my Donner und Blitzens. I realized how the Jews had suffered. Hitler was nothing to that 'tripter. I had to learn a new trade, get a new specialization. That's when I decided to get into machinery myself. Machinery plus minor surgery. Nothing overly invasive.'

He lowered his tone a little.

'Ever heard of an Erection Machine? Not likely. India's not ready for it yet I guess, or maybe getting it up is not among the marital problems you investigate? Well in the US of A that machine made it big, hah hah hah. And baby was I in the forefront of that machine! I invented it. I caught my patients by their short and curlies and they loved it. The truth is most men fail to perform just when they need to. Can't rise to the occasion. Which is one hell of an ego problem for a man, not to mention the other half lying in wait for him. It's like getting caught by the balls. Happens to all sorts of folks you'd never suspect had a problem. It's a commoner ailment than anyone lets on.'

My hands went deeper in my hip pockets.

'Well this gadget I developed solved the basic existential

problem of being born male. For a time at least. That's when I was in clover. It worked like a tiny pump. You fitted it just under the skin with a little plunger near the hip which connected with the guy's dick. He just had to pretend to scratch his hip and press the plunger a couple of times, and baby did his life begin to look up, hah hah hah. The divorce rate in Hawaii touched an all-time low. They flew me into Texas to fit up cowboys. I got calls from stud farms in Arizona. Baby was I on a high!'

In the distance I saw Shamim stagger and giggle hysterically. 'No no no Mister Alltheorie was her second husband and she discovered he was in love with Beethoven instead of her,' she said, 'so she screwed him good and proper. Ran off with his stereo. He sued her for a billion – under guess what charge?'

'What, what?' pressed her happy audience.

'High infidelity!' she screamed. They all fell about with laughter.

The dance floor was losing inhibition. Jethro Tull was singing 'Thick as a Prick'. I pressed my hips tentatively. Everything seemed in place. I felt good and relaxed.

On the larger rooftop next door another sort of party was on. There the men had moustaches, self-confidence and three-piece suits. They stood in one corner, exuding business and drinking whisky. Their women, who had accumulated layers of fat and gold jewellery, displayed these in another corner, discussing servants. There were servants in a third corner, discussing the women. Behind them all an epicene playback scratched her way through a stereo, simpering of summer with full-throated ease.

Several worlds seemed in operation, side by side. I was comfortable in mine. And the party, now that people were drunk, was clicking good as my jaw.

Pancho grinned. 'So what went wrong? I'll tell you what. The Gender Business finished me off. Was I displeased? I'll say. From technological obsolescence to disgenderizing tropes! Yes, disgenderizing trope was what they called my machine. The Gender dames in the US of A came down on me and my elevating gadget like a stone crusher. They developed abusive software to dislabel my invention. They reinvented academic jargon to kill my business. They made an academic industry out of pulverizing me. They were smart, those Gender kids. The best of them got huge salary hikes for cooking up incomprehensible essays against me which you could read backwards, sideways and upside down without changing the meaning. I got surrounded by sharks. I got reinscribed. Man I began to feel just like their prose, didn't know whether I was coming or going. There I was, all unsure the men would take to my machine and even less sure my machine would take inside my men, and suddenly I find all those chicks coming for my dick. It felt like a hit below the belt, I can tell you. The whole operation sagged. Those Gender ladies had cornered all the dough in the US of A. They lit a fire under my ass. They beat the Germans at their game. They mounted an advertising propaganda against my Erector. They sued me for mal-praxis. They called my machine a sub-text riddled with the seeds of violence. They said it was an affront to femininity. Sure it is, I said. That's the way I made it, I said. Straight up front. They didn't think that was funny in court. An assault against androgyny, they said. Sure, I said, that's what I made the machine for. They didn't like that either. A metaphoric attempt to extend the hegemony of the phallic gaze into the domain of the Other, they said. What the fuck does that mean? I asked. I got a second-order reprimand on that one. I pleaded ignorance. I tried to get into their jargon. It's enabling, I said. It's empowering, I said. It's false consciousness, they replied. That's balls, I said, it's only a fine upstanding rocket on the ready. But were they listening? It was no go on that front. My insurance company went broke. In the US of A, when a lady from insurance rings and says Baby I wouldn't touch you with a bargepole leave alone something smaller, man you better know it's Doomsday. Without insurance I couldn't fit those machines. In the anti-abortion states they were drafting legislation to outlaw my Erector alongside D&C suction pumps. I felt like a foetus. Finally the Trobriand Islanders made me an offer I couldn't refuse. They took my machines for a cut price. I cut my losses. Then I cut loose. For two years I was a headless chicken again. Then I made it to sex-change. It's a good living. Hawaii's a nice place. Come by sometime.'

I let his story swim in my system. The sea in me was all becalmed, like Hemingway on a good day. I'd never heard that sort of story in my life. In my universe there were harassed women and their struggling rescuers at one end, and my brother's crowd full of polish at the other. In my head there were oddments of drama, poetry, films and fiction. And here, somewhere in between, there was another perspective on the problems of life, sexuality, business. Pancho's problems reminded me suddenly, up on that barsati, of what Macbeth said when he was down and out and getting harassed by his lady: 'Many enterprises of great pitch and moment/ With this regard their currents turn awry/ And lose the name of action.' Or was it that Othello fellow? An image of Felicia flashed in my mind. I could feel the liquid course dimly through my guts. Possibly Hamlet. Or was it the old man who got obsolete, King Lear? I generally got mixed up on Shakespeare. All his gents were much the same. I felt my head swim. Was I Bogart or was I Wayne? Was Emperor Beethoven somewhere deep in me, and Prime Minister Nehru with a rose, tight of collar and writing elegant prose? If they deconstructed all the words that made me up would I be anyone at all? A spasm of iconoclastic disgust saved me as I lurched into a narrative mode which informed me it didn't matter. Three drinks down the line you can kick your identity crisis as high as a satellite.

Once my brother showed me Alltheorie's Gender job on Shakespeare's men. A book of five hundred leaves which said they were all much the same, all a bunch of male constructs feeling beseiged by women: wives, daughters, mothers. That book cost fifty dollars. My brother said Alltheorie made a packet out of Shakespeare. I wished I'd paid attention in school. But I was all mixed up. Inside me Shakespeare's lines floated like reckless fish in a chaotic sea. Now and then they came like unexpected whales into

111

the novels of my mind, harbouring in stray areas of the sandbanks that were my identities. There they lodged for a time, as snug as pencils in the ears of carpenters. I generally knew what Shakespeare's men felt and said, and their words still described Pancho's predicament better than I could. *Plus ça change, plus c'est la même chose.*

Pancho and I exchanged cards. He was lucky I was his sole audience. I could think of people in the rest of the crowd who wouldn't have taken his story quite as pleasantly as I did. My brother, for instance. He got furious every time he thought anyone was belittling his profession with plebeian words. He and his guests had investments in the empire where Alltheorie was queen.

'Okay,' I said to him once, choosing my words with care to offset his. 'I'm strictly on the outside. You and I went to different schools. We learned English syntax from different books. Your new queen's English came out of France. Okay, so time's winged chariot crossed the Channel since I left school.'

Recently, it had begun to seem to me that we were differently constituted, a passing phase maybe, which called for coexistence, not quarrel. My brother and I levelled on that. What if we spoke in different tongues? Blood is thicker than words. In the detection business it's important to keep a sceptical distance from these emotion industries where people play games with words. The world of anger and telegrams, sound and fury, sexuality and its Other. They weren't going to suck me in like they were sucking in my brother. Look at Holmes, Trent, Marple, Marlowe, Dalgleish, Poirot. They don't get sucked in. They listen to the stories they're told. They just listen. Their investments in narrative are strictly intellectual. Their connections are eccentric. Like mine. No emotion, just intellect plus eccentricity equalling a modest living. In our business that's the sure way to avoid muddle, end mystery. It's the straight and narrow for us privates. And thereby hangs a dick.

Pancho was grinding his cigarette under his heel. I looked at my watch. The booze had shifted the weather out of my subcutaneous. I felt uplifted like the clouds, as buoyant as Bogart, as regal as Nehru, as laid back as Wayne. I raised my sombrero a notch, in the way one does when one bids *adiós* to an hombre in the Wild West. It was late.

'Well,' I said to Pancho, 'I'll know who to contact if I want to pee sitting down. For now I've got to do it standing up, hah hah hah. Let's get together soon.'

Shamim's little girl was curled up in sleep near the water tank. Pancho saw her at the same moment.

'Let's tuck her into bed,' I said.

He helped me lift the little girl and put her on the divan in the quieter room. I put a sheet over the kid. She was a sweet kid. It was okay to feel something for her. Kids were generally straight. They cut out the crap and said their piece straight. I saw Pancho give her a little peck on my way out. He was okay, that doc. My brother and his crowd would have thought different, but he liked kids. I wasn't wrong about him. That was my first nice party.

Business picked up over the days after that nice party. I was soon back in my own world, floating idly through the currents of different words till I was brought ashore to my own easy vocabulary by the call of business. The phone came alive with a woman who was married to a high-up cop. She suspected him of spending time away from home above and beyond the call of duty. She was one of many. Women like her were okay. Their hunches were mostly right. They wanted their guys to shoot from the hip and spoke straight. They gave me business. Here there were no words to waste.

I tailed the cop for three days. Each day he'd hit the jail, thrash a couple of dozen undertrials to keep them hopping, come out refreshed, then head straight for his lady love in a house close by. I gave his legal wife the address which affronted her womanhood and three colour pictures. She gave me three grand for the info. In my experience the pudding always came after the proof.

I felt secure in my world, anchored by silence and straight speech. I preferred this to my brother's world, with its superfluity of nuances, its infinite problematizations of settled notions, its glorifications of subjective experience, its negations of the truth, its uncertainties and its angsts larded in the jargon of the large-salaried. All the same I liked getting the gen on his world for it gave perspective to mine. A different point of view. He valued me for much the same.

So, in the months that followed I visited my brother to see how he was doing in his struggles with history, and on one of these visits I found him looking baffled and unkempt, his hair in a Beethoven mess and papers scattered all over the barsati floor. He said he'd been attending a course in Alltheorie and found she swam too fast for little fish like him to keep up. He looked like a pair of ragged claws scuttling across the floors of volatile seas. George Eliot? Could have been T.S. Either way, he couldn't keep up with Alltheorie. Even though, he said, she was reputed to be off colour, in a manner of speaking: she was in a state of extreme depression.

'Extreme depression? How come?' I asked.

'Take a look at this,' he said, pointing me to a paper on the floor. I picked up a leaflet and began reading:

In their preoccupation with the palatable forms of popular culture, all students of the peasantry except Lavatri Alltheorie have neglected an important arena of peasant existence, namely the history of belching, wind-breaking and defecation.

To name these functions in this order – belching, farting, shitting – is to posit a sociological hierarchy, a bourgeois hierarchy of disgust with what Marx termed 'The Asiatic Commode of Production'.

I shall not consider an important secondary peasant function, namely sweating, because this site has been explored by Alltheorie in 'Faces and Faeces: Peasant Expressions During Evacuation', and 'The Crap Trap: Peasants and Acute

Constipation'; and because the historian's concern, as Alltheorie demonstrates, is not with India's toiling millions but with its toileting millions . . .

Subsection 1: The Holy Cow of Sociology: What I term 'udder displacement' has very considerable consequences, first for gender, second for sociology, and third for the cow. With its udder displaced in the proportion Three is to Two, the cow lets forth a gush of Alltheorienne wind, which, mediated through sociology, reaches the ears of our somnolent peasant, who delivers upon his female kin a kick each which reverberates first through gender and then most strikingly upon the physiognomic space commonly designated in the vocabulary of the vulgar as 'The Arse'.

This privileged intervention . . .

I gave up at that point. The only cows I understood were the ones which jelled in the frost, ate newspapers for breakfast, and shared my vaulting ambition to quit this wicked world by going over the moon and joining the satellites. Here there was a whole new universe of lowing herds winding their way o'er a sociological lea, and baby, it put the wind up me to read that prose. I sensed a hostile edge within its humour. It seemed funny in a convoluted way, but it wasn't altogether endearing. It confirmed there were seaweeds in my brother's pool waiting with their jaws wide. Even the mighty fish got bits of their underbellies nipped. It raised a laugh, but equally it deepened my image of the world. It didn't matter whether you had big words in your armoury like Alltheorie and my brother's crowd, or words that were vulgar and little like the ones in Pancho's erection therapy or my detection business. Either way, there was a world outside trying to get in with the weather, waiting to get you when you stepped out. You survived or went under.

Of course my brother didn't find it funny at all. He worshipped that lady. She was like Elizabeth Taylor for his prose, not Forster, not Nehru, not Orwell neither. If you couldn't get your pen doing a half-Nelson, you weren't an academic acrobat. The paycheck was low if you didn't write it right. Without verbal pyrotechnics you were liable to a cut in salary at the end of the month. To make it big he had to make his words bigger. So what if it killed meaning? Bad writing? Big deal. He'd bought himself a dic loaded with academic jargon to uplift his career graph. The world was full of big fish. To stay afloat you had to keep switching software. Like Pancho. Like my brother the historian.

'That parody's been circulating all over the University,' he said in an anxious way. 'First she was hopping mad and wanted to get at the author. Then she got depressed because she's been lecturing all the time about the fact that texts don't really have authors you can pinpoint. Now she doesn't know what to do. She's feeling undermined.'

'I should think so,' I said, greasing my face with false sympathy and switching to my business software. 'Maybe she needs a private dick,' I said.

For a moment my brother looked disgusted. He kicked some papers on the floor, but then he looked reflective and exclaimed: 'Hey maybe that's not such a bad idea.'

My brother was a slow thinker. He was always slow coming. He started life that way. I came out of our mum before you could say labour. He took so long they had to do a Rush Caesar. He was a minor historian. You could see why.

I kept my cards close to my chest and gave him one of them to pass on to his idol. 'In case she needs a dick,' I said.

Four straying-men days later I'm in my Lowdown Dick mode, jes sittin' in my office doing a blow job on the phone to make it come alive when in walks this replica of my picture theory of reality. One among my many mental concepts with two legs and some-thing good betwixt. Not exactly Liz Taylor, but going on Marlene Dietrich. Same husky voice. The voice of a lady once a gent. She puts my card on the table and gets to the point with a personifi-cation that makes me reach for my hip pockets.

'Hello sweetheart,' she says in just my kind of language, 'I believe you're something I badly need.'

I'm grateful for trousers with pockets. At first I look wary. Then I give her my chewing-gum detachment stare. This doesn't distract her any. 'C'mon cowboy,' she says affably, like she's fondled me from the cradle, 'I need to chew the cud with you. They tell me you've got the goods! There's something I badly need, and you look like you've got it.'

By now my jaw muscles have given up on the gum routine and Existentialism's getting them down. I find it incredible that the lady speaks my vocabulary so swell she's practically inside my identity.

'Like what?' I ask nervously. My fingers do a clutch-and-shuffle deep in my epistemology.

'A private . . . er, detective, I believe?'

She smiles a smile and we talk. About This, That and the Other.

'My first detective. I've never had any sort of experience with privates before.'

By now she's got me relaxed. 'Well Professor,' I reply with a grin, 'I hope I've got what you're looking for.'

She laughs wickedly. I grin some more. Very pleasant. No condescension. No big words. A suppressed sense of humour. I like her. Her figure helps. After a while the conversation gets so charming it makes me loosen my belt a notch. My epidermis reacts well to her atmosphere. An aroma straight out of France. Chanel No. 5.

'This is No. 2,' says Lavatri. 'I know your sweetheart brother has already shown you No. 1.' She hands me a leaflet. 'I'm looking for the author of this rotten prose,' she says, and then compounds the mystery with a high-theoretical aside: 'that is, in the unlikely event that such texts can possibly have an author.'

I pay no attention to her aside. I'm in business. If she wants an author, an author is what I aim to get her. I pick up the leaflet and read some more serious frivolity:

In Bengal, in the beginning was the Words, and the Words was Tagore and Bankim (pronounced Bonk'im). Nothing much existed before Tagore and Bonk'im, except Bengal. But the chicken-and-egg debate among Bengali intellectuals has taken the form of arguing over what came first – Tagore and Bonk'im, or Bengal. Alltheorie's admirers say she has taken the correct view, namely that all life is made up of socially constructed and gendered semiotic signs, from which it follows that Tagore and Bonk'im must have come first.

She also specially reinscribes Bonk'im as India's first third-rate prose writer, the subaltern who unified all Englishmen in the use of a single expression – Bonk'im.

Alltheorie's detractors argue that Bonk'im derives not from Bonk Him but from the word Bunkum, for Bengal's most sacred text the *Oxford English Dictionary* refers to the *Collected Works of Bonk'im* as *Bonk'im's Complete Bunkum*, specifically to the edition prepared by Alltheorie, who is renowned for her specialization in Complete Bunkum.

This is the discursive double-helix of modern Indian history. Alltheorists follow the neo-Taylorian managerial imperialist Henry Ford, who said 'All History is Bonk'im'. Following this axiom, the historian of modern India now dwells on the grammar of the colonial rape of countryside natives. If Macaulay recorded the lays of ancient Rome, Indian historians are busy recording the laying of modern India . . .

There was a whole lot more after that, but I'd had enough: it had the mordant tone of the earlier one, suggesting an author very much in the singular. My brother would have understood the prose better and been appalled. For a change I found myself in sympathy with him, largely and most mysteriously because I seemed to have warmed to the character under fire.

That was the most astounding thing about the whole business. I'd started off with a heavy load of prejudice against that lady and seen, all of a sudden, my preconceptions about her dissolve within an instant of her real-life presence. It happens that way sometimes, just when you're expecting different. From what I'd heard about Lavatri Alltheorie, I'd expected my skin to go into a crawl, whereas there it lay under my phallic gaze, all lambent and risible. It confirmed my view that human reactions are about as accountable as the next day's weather – globally, cross-culturally.

'Lavatri,' I say, 'I can't say I understand all the nuances in these defamous pamphlets, but if you're looking for information on their author, do tell your Swiss bankers to send me a crossed cheque for a million.'

Lavatri laughs most becomingly, a laughter amazingly like Pancho's which makes me feel easy with my own set of words. I wonder if she's come in chase of an author or her first experience with a private dick. I relax and regress entirely to my limited vocabulary, my own comfortable patterns of thought, quite pleasantly nonplussed by her unexpected ease in the vocabulary of conversational charm. She wears a saree through which my fingers could traverse the history of the Silk Route, reaching an oasis where the caravan of my identities might merge into a singular climax. I scent a body odour from over the Channel and gaze at a mouth that takes you from here to eternity. I have to hand it to her.

Some other day, some other place.

We agree on an undisclosable sum. I get the job.

That case was the most intellectual thing I ever did in my entire life. I combed the universities for linguists to decipher those leaflets and give me clues. I learned a whole lot from them – all about transformed grammar and Chompsky hamburgers. I left hungry for more. So I got going on professors of literary theory who might have info on the parodist. They were supposed to be adept at deconstructing texts. They were all at conferences in California and came back clueless. So I chased librarians. They'd never seen a book in their lives.

In between I met Lavatri, first in my office, then in surroundings more congenial, and to confess the truth I found us coming uncomfortably close. She was charming, she was nice, she was replete with every sort of narrative. I discovered to my considerable surprise and extreme discomfort that despite all my respect for professional theories of investigation, Lavatri's many stories, the undeniability of her real-life presence, and the specific odour of her armpits, which reminded me of a pianist descended of Liszt undoing a pearl necklace, all made me want to get sucked in. At first I justified my attraction to her by attributing it, in the way of Amma who was so stuffed full of literary complexes, to my Tiresias Complex, the desire for intellectual knowledge of a lady once a gent. Wasn't that how my brother felt? But gradually I was forced to face a less comfortable truth: my physiology was telling my epistemology to take a walk or get stuffed. Or was ours the attraction of a shared identity crisis, a mutual desire to merge with the Other out of a radical uncertainty of Self? I realized what it must have taken for her to experiment physiologically with identity; it put in perspective the caution of my own mental experiments as well as the limited self-definitions which most people accepted to keep their ships on an even keel. And so, as I spent more time with her, I gradually came to agree with Lavatri Alltheorie that life and identity seemed mainly made up of a plethora of questions and problems, a complex range of causes with no reassuring answers. I tried to resist her subversion of my preconceptions, my essential selfhood: nothing worked. I felt like a peasant facing a landlady. The more I saw her, smelt the air around her and heard her voice with its undertow of strong arguments, the more I watched helplessly as my earlier notions dissolved along with my resistance. Like my brother's crowd I aspired to her words, and to all that lay beneath. I felt the secure sandbank of my essential being licked by the tidal wave of her Master Narrative. I felt destined for the deep.

Then, just about the time that things seemed building up to an enormous identity crisis, I hit upon a feminist press full of ladies poring over manuscripts and my parodies rang a bell in one of the editors.

'I think I remember that style,' she said. 'It looks like the early Bhaiya-Sabko. Professor Gyandeo Bhaiya-Sabko offered us an anthology of parodies many years ago, long before he became famous. We couldn't publish it because it had no footnotes. It may even have been libellous.'

Did that strike a gong in me! Did I whistle when I heard that! I'd reckoned on professional jealousy as the motive of crime against Alltheorie but I'd stumbled on a bonus: this backstabbing looked like domestic jealousy with attempted regicide. It seemed straight out of *Hamlet*. It could have been *Macbeth*. How about the Chou-Mao bayonet which went right through Nehru? Take a look at *King Lear*. How about *Othello*? Does it matter?

My lady editor fished for a long while in her drawers. I watched with bated breath for the naked truth to appear. She was nice to look at. I wished I was visiting in some other capacity. But I wasn't.

She pulled out another parody. I groaned. I felt trapped. Luckily it was only a fragment.

. . . the function of modern parody, in line with contemporary theoretical enterprises, is to contest what has been canonized. Academics engaged in 'canon-firing' have now themselves been canonized; they have, moreover, canonized an academic prose-style so full of arcane jargon that it makes every sane woman wince. Therefore, our parodies are inspired by Indian historians and feminist intellectuals (these being more or less the same thing). Collectively they represent a cannon aimed most specifically at destabilizing and hopefully sinking the newly canonized academic and the hideousness of her prose style.

These new Alltheoreticiennes take themselves and what they spout very seriously. Fortunately their seminal outpourings are frequently verbal on account of India's preference for the oral tradition, and, being unfailingly delivered in Bengali, mostly to each other, can be happily ignored as passing verbiage . . .

121

'I can trust you to keep that confidential?' said the lady editor. She didn't say that in the imperative mood. She didn't frame that like a rhetorical question. There weren't metaphors in her syntax, nor no synecdoches neither. She said it straight like a fact. She wasn't circular. She had a nice figure. The vibes were good between us. I thought I'd visit her in some other capacity.

Some other place, some other time.

'You can,' I said. I thanked her for the info. I was in my best Bogart mood, with just a touch of Poirot. Deadpan gallantry. We smiled at each other in the way that suggests a future life. Her shape looked good. But my job called for no emotion beyond a warm thank-you smile. She'd given me as much as I wanted. For that day.

My investigative narrative had reached a neat climax. The jigsaw sentences of those parodies had an author behind them whose existence Lavatri, of all people, could not possibly doubt. I saw for myself that Professor Gyandeo Bhaiya-Sabko had jack-knifed his way into the very core of her being, that every text had an author if only you penetrated the matter hard.

As soon as I discovered she'd been cut to the quick in that Shakespearean way by her own lover – one of my pre-texts, if that's the phrase – I went across to Lavatri's and told her the objective truth about the missing narrator as gently as I could, in accordance with the dictates of my profession which had now got so deeply complicit with my non-allergic response to her statu-esque charm.

At first she wouldn't believe me. So I showed her a photocopy of the fragment. Then, to my surprise, she laughed and said, 'Never mind, sweetheart. Maybe it's better to go on believing that texts don't really have authors. But thanks anyway, and why don't you sit down and take off some of your excess clothes.'

I was stumped, having expected my investigation to undo some of *her* fundamental truths for a change, or at least shake her up, but she was entirely resilient and had switched to the romantic mode. I felt another change of vocabulary overcome me. As I threw my professional identity with all its accoutrements off with my clothes and saw my feelings for her rise beyond a permissible professional point, I recalled myself as the celibate shikari Jim Corbett who, with his gun ready for a tigress, unexpectedly encountered a beautiful Austrian woman pianist in the jungles of his mind. 'Are you game?' cried the hunter in confusion. 'Sure I'm game,' cried back the piano lady. Upon this Corbett threw off his celibate mind, saw only a dense jungle ahead, raised his gun, took careful aim, and let her have it.

Of course Lavatri would have described the same thing much better. In her tongue, it could be said that I got sucked, imbricated and intertextualized like a spasmodic sub-text into the deepest ontological recesses of her liquid Master Narrative.

If I didn't admire the telegraphic style, if I wasn't hampered by Nehru and Hemingway, I would describe it better. But there are occasions for which silence says it all. Those are the narratives for which one has no words at all.

Lavatri and I saw each other several times after that, but as generally happens with sudden and unexpected relationships, once the novelty wears thin there's a whole world pulling you in one direction and her in another. Slowly, inevitably, that world too lost colour and weakened into an opaque grey film and so, despite our new-found respect for each other and the short but furious closeness of our contact, we lost touch.

Some months after I handed over that confidential information, I heard from my brother that she'd quit Lit.Clit. No one knew the real reason. There weren't any real reasons left in history. Only questions, hypotheses, theories, no answers.

'That woman never seems short of surprises though, that's for sure,' said my brother. 'I met her yesterday and she said she wants to find her roots in Bengal to understand Tagore and Bankim. She says she knows inside herself it can't be done without being in the right gender. So d'you know what she's decided on doing?'

I didn't, but to my astonishment I found myself saying 'Yes', impelled by some obscure, involuntary impulse. I watched helpless and felt the words escape out of my mouth. Sometimes I really don't know the words that come out of me at all, they just come out of me on their own:

'She's fishing for a good doc to do a reverse sex-change operation on her.'

My brother looked aghast. 'So you've heard?' he asked.

'No,' I said. 'I think I just had a premonition.'

That was the naked truth. Despite what I learned from Lavatri I think sometimes there's some kind of essential reality that brews in me like it does inside the witches' cooking pot in one of those Shakespearean tragedies, and occasionally, unaccountably, the steam escapes out of me in the shape of words. On such occasions, as on those when I fail for words, I watch this reality as it forms without feeling in control even of my own words. I don't know how this happens, it just does. It's as though life wants all the time to subvert my theories and sometimes puts words into my mouth that I didn't even know were there. I find myself saying things I didn't even know I knew, possessing identities of which I had only the faintest suspicion and getting to know them when they've spilled out of me on their own, like a smile or a laugh or a cry of anguished pleasure.

'Well,' said my brother, looking at me long and hard, 'Lavatri sounded serious. It's unbelievable. It must be something personal. I mean it can't be just professional like she's making it sound.'

He paused, standing there by his water tank, pulling reflectively at his cigarette and recalling inside me an image from that nice party. I think sometimes my whole being strives to make impossible connections and yearns to string together things that seem inconceivably far from each other, like Nehru and Beethoven, like Elizabeth Taylor and Ivan Karamazov, like Hemingway and Shakespeare, or like . . .

'Lavatri and Pancho,' said my brother, snatching the words out of my head. 'D'you remember Pancho? Well this time round I'm fixing for Lavatri to meet him. Can you believe that? She's a research perfectionist. So she wants to be a man again!'

So she's moving from a dick to a doc, I thought, then corrected my syntax. So she needs a dick from a doc.

Lavatri meeting Pancho! Jesus! I'd cared for them both in nicely different ways, but the combination sounded lethal. It sounded to me like an announcement for the Day of Judgement in the gender business.

Not that I cared to forecast the future. My own experience of the difference between the winds of theory and the concrete occurrences of real life suggested something more like an imminent coupling, a possibly happy coming together in the gender trade. That'll make some Master Narrative, I thought.

Some other time, some other place.

It was late in the afternoon and the December clouds were coming in low outside, swift and slowing grey. I saw them gather to a dark intensity and soon a winter drizzle began to slant against the windowpanes of my brother's barsati. It drummed hard against the arresting glass, and somewhere in the atmosphere beyond I caught the aroma of sibling rivalry. I looked at my watch. It was time to leave.

As my windscreen wipers slashed the sky I watched once more an evocative rain. I recalled an old man in a frail boat and a fisherman's lakeside miracles, I saw Lady Macbeth with blood on her hands, I resurrected Ophelia from the Dead Sea and made her waltz on water, I heard the music of Cordelia's voice soothe the turbulent sea in Othello, I made Nehru buttonhole Beethoven with a red rose, I counted my indentities and reached the sun of infinity, and then, just like hickory-dickory, as clearcut as a nursery rhyme or a mix or memories you don't deconstruct, as straight as the affection you feel for a girl, I remembered the distant, silent stars over that evening party when Shamim's little daughter, whose cousin Divya joined the K.G.'B', fell asleep curled up by a water tank.

7

Incident by the Pangong Lake

My brother, who resembled Zeus and later Beethoven, was once sitting by the Pangong Lake in eastern Ladakh, quietly breathing in the scant and icy air at fourteen thousand feet. He watched a black dot which was really a yak disappear through an afternoon into a cream-coloured hill that froze over a navy-blue lake which stretched itself out all the way to Tibet, and he wondered with slow thought, as people sometimes do, why it seemed so aesthetically pleasing to him to be sitting there all alone, just watching the water.

There wasn't much to do except just silently gaze at the water and feel heroic. He watched the water with slit Clint Eastwood eyes and imagined his heroic face with its desirable stubble, and his slim, long figure, all being watched with a mixture of tenderness and unadmitted desire by Shabana Azmi, the always unreachable movie heroine of his frequent mental wanderlust. He looked at the lake and she, the forever lovely Grecian-Urn beloved of his mind, watched him. Once or twice he made her sigh quietly with desire. It amused him that he could in his own mind revel in a power play which so fluently allowed a complete reversal of their real-life positions. The knowledge that he had a permanent inner capacity to make himself her hero provided him with a deep and wholesome satisfaction. It gave him a strong sense of his own being, and because he had the intelligence to recognize this power as an aspect of a narcissism he cherished, he could control or restrain it at will, or alternatively allow it to swamp his insides with all the hormones of lust.

He grinned happily to himself at the attractiveness of the scenario his mind had constructed, felt vaguely sorry once more that there was no one to thank for an imagination that bestowed him with images that came like sudden, unexpected gifts, and smiled at the thought of a safely distant feminist circle which frowned in conjunction at the hideous maleness of all the operations of his mind. He tried to focus on specific faces within his feminist circle, looking for something undogmatic and physically desirable behind the cigarette smoke of hardening expressions. There were possibilities, but by that navy-blue lake, at that moment, it seemed too tiring to pursue this train of thought towards a passionate conclusion. It took only a split second to file away his feminist circle. It felt nice to know his mind filed faster than his personal computer as he switched, he thought, to another software.

The world looked good, and nothing bothered him there, by that lake. The sounds of horns and motorcars belonged to another universe as he let the alchemy of silence and spectacle slowly flood his veins towards the experience of a harmony that, elsewhere, within the cities of noise where he was often forced to make a living, came to him with the power of a narcotic through the 'Emperor' Concerto and certain slow movements in old symphonies. There was an eternal tranquillity to the lake and the colours around my brother were more bizarre and compelling than any to be seen in Dali. It required no exceptional imagination – merely the barest topographical realism in fact – for a writer to paint with words a world as extraordinary as any to be found in Màrquez. The hills slanted sharply up in spasms of strange colour, cream and black and green, and the maroon of garnets lay muffled in their stones. They formed a new conjunction with the full moon which was nearly as lucid as a sun that dipped on the opposite hill and coloured the lake towards a lighter shade of grey. The slow meanderings of my brother's mind as he watched this scene were an analogue of his unencumbered travels through the valleys and passes of Manali, Lahul and Spiti, to the point where he sat upon garnet stones by the Pangong Lake, constructing in his mind the pleasing images of an impossible relationship.

It was here that, stirred by the sweep of the Pangong Lake, a new run of images began to crystallize in my brother's mind. He tried to sort out these images towards a narrative which would convey with some exactness the circumstances that culminated in his being there, by the purple beach, but he discovered, even as he thought, that there were many alternative histories inside him which concluded in his position by that lake-water lapping with low sounds upon a high and remote shore. There was at one level a dull and circumstantial history, the shallow rehearsal of recent physical activities: the coughing back-kick of a cold motorcycle flinching to the downward arc of a feeble and wind-bitten leg, the dry lips and the dark glasses below a warm helmet, the donning of gloves and the revving sounds which soothed his heartbeat, the drooping yellow of willow trees that hid the pale blue flow of the Indus near Leh, the clicked gears and the passing blackness of a bare road which snaked its way through deserted mountains and the tongues of glaciers towards the lake.

This seemed one way of telling the truth about how he got to that altitude of colours: he had evidence and no doubt. But there seemed an infinity of other narratives which served as interesting preludes to his view upon that chromatic afternoon of a disappearing yak, images to be tracked along unexpected contours, all waiting to be ordered by a distinctive and personal logic into a history which defined only his own soul. The water reminded him, as he kick-started a mental motorbike, of the colour of his old school blazer and a day, twenty years earlier, when his blazer accidentally tore upon a nail and was freed by a boy who, some days later, ran away from the school. It took him to his own construction of that boy, Vincente de Rozio, who, dislodging his blazer from a nail, asked him on that day, all those many years in the past, 'Hey men, you ever seen the Pangong Lake?'

Our horizons were small in those days. Our school lay by a beautiful ox-bow lake, cut off before our time from a river that flowed dimly in the distance, and we had seen the bigger lakes of Naini Tal, Bhim Tal and Srinagar when our parents herded us there to save our skins the annual baking that began in earnest after the first week of May. There were other lakes, much larger, Chilka, Titicaca, Michigan, that filled our minds with the notion of an enormous tranquillity. Even the smaller stretches of water we encountered in our city – the mud-brown ponds circumscribed by mud huts where buffaloes sank with the barest trace of their nostrils, and the river that swayed every evening through the shadows of decaying palaces – even these seemed havens of rest, cool islands of refuge from the blaze of bicycle traffic and horns that pursued us through every street of our city. Though we did not know it then, my brother said later he realized most fully, sitting by the Pangong Lake, how deep the feeling for a bounded expanse of water had sunk into our minds. The calmness and colour of that water belonged to a better world than ours. Or perhaps I should say, more truthfully, that they belonged to a better world than mine, for my brother was less held up by the routine pleasures of family and friends, and he was able to travel and live in worlds that I could only strain to imagine.

To de Rozio my brother said, twenty years before his reconstruction of that event – No, he hadn't heard of this lake, what was this Pangong Lake? He remembered the quirky comparison Vincente made when he said the lake was bloody large and looked like it was all made of blazer cloth. He said it was half in Ladakh and half in Tibet. His father's regiment, said Vincente, was posted at Tankse, an army outpost not far from the lake, and he'd seen it floating about amid the colour of the mountains after a five-hour ride through yak-dotted terrain which seemed to have been specially set apart from human beings.

A few days later Vincente de Rozio ran away from the school, and for many years out of my brother's life, until he found him coming alive in his mind because of a torn blazer and the purple of the Pangong Lake. He thought back to the time when de Rozio fled the school and recalled it as an incident which, like the tranquillity and colour of the lake that lay before him, liberated his mind from the certitudes on which we were all being fed, on all the home truths which made the majority of us, in our adult lives, captives to office and a pressure-cooker domesticity. It was one of the things, he said, that made him a traveller. I think he meant by this that it made him emotionally and intellectually restless, for he didn't physically travel until quite long after our years in school and much after the de Rozio incident. But the incident freed him somehow. It informed him, in the odd and obscure way in which these things inform the subconscious and only later assume the shape of links within a pattern, that he didn't have to receive the truths on which we were being educated. The possibility of dissent, the possibility that we were being schooled on lies or values that weren't universal truths, the possibility of a spectacular and radical denial of authority – these seemed all to coalesce in his recollection of de Rozio and the circumstances in which he fled the school. It was an image he couldn't dissociate, within the convolutions of his mind, from the fact that he himself had become restless and a traveller.

We were both sceptical about what constituted truth and reality and value: they seemed to shift so much from day to day, depending on the weather, the topography and the temperature of our bodies, that we had become attuned to believing in the more acceptably uncertain virtues and disappointments we encountered in friendship, fiction and music.

My brother went much further in this direction than I. He moved around the world with such dogged restlessness and with such little interest in material ambition that the worldly-wise knew him only as a shiftless tramp. His whole life seemed a negation of all that they had been taught to valorize – consistency, purposiveness, possessions, an ordered life in a safe city which assured a position, a pension, a provident fund. My brother would have none of these. He liked looking at lakes and the water of different countries. He loved women all over the world for the short periods of time he stayed with them, then moved on and loved other people, other sights, picking up the threads easily from just where he'd left them every time he circumnavigated his way back to an old haunt or a far-flung friend. He valorized movement, newness, change, a purposiveness without purpose which I could only envy. He sought out lakes and the stretches of water on which his eyes could feast and rest, but even here his mind was mostly on the move, travelling backwards and forwards on a train of images, some recollected, others constructed, all equally real because they appeared gathered together into an experience of immediate and transient value, to be cherished because they could not recur in the same shape, near the same expanse of water, at that precise temperature and altitude. So my brother didn't know, nor much cared, how that important little incident of his past *really* happened. But this is how I think he made history happen inside himself, sitting by the Pangong Lake.

Late on an October night towards the close of the 1960s, in our biggish city which lay prostrate upon the Gangetic plain of north India, Vincente de Rozio, fourteen years old and an obscure descendant of certain Portuguese merchants who once lived in Goa, made his escape down a drainpipe from a school that had quartered him for much of his life. His heart raced in his ears as he made his tentative way down the rough edges of a rusting pipe towards the ground, where three cast-iron cannons, fired once by Lord Cornwallis against Tipu Sultan, now pointed the direction to an ox-bow lake in which seven crocodiles had made their home, being shot and logged one at a time over seven mythical years by Colonel Townsend, the old school principal with a dictator's moustache who once placed an order for one small Gandhi on the phone.

Fearing detection and inching quietly down the thirty feet, Vincente de Rozio did not notice – as my brother did then, creating the scene – the fading moon, slit here and there by arrow clouds and shining upon the ox-bow lake a hundred yards away. It only took Vincente de Rozio five minutes of ear-ache and sore thighs to feel his black Bata pointed shoes touch ground. He looked up and sideways to make sure he was alone and safe before beginning his walk over the low school gate, over the culvert that ran over an arm of the lake, over the fifth hole of the golf course, across Fairy Dale and towards the limp flag of the third hole, on to the Dilkusha Gardens, and finally beyond the restless city's sleep towards the Civil Lines.

Questions about where de Rozio went from there and what ultimately became of him were asked every day for several months, by all the schoolboys, soon after the news got around that he had run away. No one could recollect an instance of such spectacular rebellion. If you couldn't answer the questions that were asked in class, it was logical to expect a beating to follow. Some beatings were merely savager than others – it depended partly on the master whose questions you blanked out on. If it was history, you had no time. The history master looked black as a panther, weighed more than Muhammad Ali, had a nasty temper, a pencil moustache that went too far in both directions before dipping menacingly, a wife with whom his relations were rapidly souring, and an unending sequence of children who all said Daddy Daddy with gratuitous regularity and without adequate cause. Given this, it was unlikely to benefit your scholarly destiny if you were prone to confusing, as de Rozio was, the Chandlers of Bundlecund with the Rohillers of Rohillcund.

An exact scene grew within my brother's mind as he gazed towards Tibet, vaguely connecting the silence there with the one into which de Rozio had disappeared. It began with the period bell which rang out the time for history to start, followed by the arrival into the class of the Black Panther, his moustache twitching, his mouth in a shape which gave out the unfilial echoes of Daddy Daddy, his face with an expression that suggested considerable marital deterioration since the last lesson, in his hand a cane which he placed on the desk in front of him.

'Wake up ya buggers.'

That sounded quite normal to the class: it was the Panther's favoured way of combining a greeting with a warning and seemed to call for no special wariness.

'Albert ya bugger.'

'Yessir,' said Albert Joel Kumar Menezes.

'Your bloody dad is in the bloody army, ya bugger, and I have to buy rum in the bloody market. How d'you think you're going to pass in history, Albert? No rum, no marks, heh heh heh. Just tell your dad to send his batman to the canteen and get me some rum ya bugger. *Hum bloody paisa déga man, but tum bloody rum kab bring karéga?*'

'I'll bring by Monday sir, pukka sir.'

'You heard that, bloody Vincente de Rozio? You're another useless worthless bugger I say. Do you bloody know what bloody Portugal is most famous for? Port, ya bugger, port. Not bloody port like bloody Bombay and Madras and all men, port inside bottles. Port-oo-bloody-gull. And have you ever had the basic decency to get me a bloody bottle from your bloody native land? My birthday's coming up next month, ya buggers, and you know how I like to celebrate, heh heh heh. Look sharp bloody de Rozio, I don't want any of your bloody Latin looks or I'll give you such a bloody kick you'll land in bloody Lisbon with your grand-daddies.'

It was suddenly hot. The boys in the class shifted uneasily in their chairs and glanced from de Rozio to the Panther. It was incredible for de Rozio to have looked anything but placating: there was no precedent for sullenness and rebellion in history until then, my brother said. The world did not exist outside the class, the violence of its atmosphere holding everyone tightly captive. A strangulating blackness which struck deeper than fear had closed every mind against the worlds which lay outside, where there was movement and the calmness of lakes. The Panther's mood was unmistakable and my brother knew, with the certitude of the habitually defeated, that success in history only meant humouring a regularly dangerous animal. Later, when he came across Carlyle's remark that the only thing man ever learnt from history was that man never learnt anything from history, my brother thought it applied very ironically to de Rozio who, on that day, seemed to think of the history period as one in which we were meant to learn history. Perhaps de Rozio had suddenly and unaccountably developed more expectations of education than the rest of us; or perhaps the intellectual sickness which was as characteristic of our school as its physical charm struck him suddenly on that day, so many years before my brother and I were able to see it that way; or perhaps he was better equipped than we had guessed with the special thickness of mind and skin that served well as a strategy for survival in our school; or perhaps he just had less to lose by being defiant. Whatever it was, no one who was present in that class ever forgot what followed. The Panther said the topic for the day was . . .

'Aurangzeb the bugger. I'll give you his story in the form of a . . .'

'Skeleton, sir,' said the boys dutifully.

'And you will go back home and fill in the . . .'

'Flesh, sir,' said the boys dutifully. Vincente de Rozio's voice was not heard in the chorus. He was looking straight at the Panther.

'Now, as I hope yoll buggers already know, Aurang bloody zeb, son of Shah bloody Jahan, was the last of the pukka Mughal emperors. And do yoll know why he was the last in that first batch of cutcock emperors? No, yoll don't! And why not? Because I haven't yet told yoll! Heh heh heh. *Now,* I'll tell yoll why. You see, one of Aurangzeb the bugger's problems was transport,' said the Panther. 'No bloody motorcars and all men, only bloody horses. Big buggers. Huge buggers. Big huge bloody horses. By the time Aurangzeb the bugger put on his armour and sword and shield and all, his bloody horse was ready to sit down. So

134

Aurangzeb couldn't bloody move, ya buggers. Besides it was too hot for the bugger. Bloody Mughals had come straight from Summercund, I say, nonstop kitapit kitapit kitapit kitapit on their horses. Everyone told the buggers India was the land of bloody milk and honey. No one told the buggers about our bloody milkmen I say. Bloody Arjun Kumar I thought your dad was going to send us fresh milk from last week on men, what happened eh? You want to bloody fail in history just like bloody Albert or what men? Just remember. So what was I saying, yes, by the time it was bloody Aurang's turn to be Emperor, his blood ran dry with the heat I say. Look up Summercund in your maps for the next class, ya buggers, that's the hideout from which all those chinky-eyed cutcocks came, from Genghis Khan to Tamer bloody Lane to our own haircutting Babur heh heh heh. Straight line of descent to Aurang bloody zeb. So what was I saying? Yeah, Aurangzeb the bugger. Everything was hot and heavy I say. Bugger must have cursed bloody Babur for bloody leaving Summercund and landing him in this land of bloody milk and water. Bloody Arjun Kumar I hope my gentle hints heh heh are not lost inside your thick skull. Yes, so Aurang bloody zeb. His cannons were heavy, all full of balls and all men. Everything was heavy ya buggers. Bloody Mughals had got used to booze and dames by the time they got to Aurang I say. Even their horses, men, heh heh heh. Empire was bloody decaying. When you feel like lying around with some booze and your horse doesn't feel like bloody moving either, what can you do, I say. What d'you think about all these things Albert ma boy? You don't think, Albert ma boy. That's the trouble with you, Albert ma boy. I'll tell you what Aurangzeb did, Albie ma boy. He just said bye bye to his empire, just bye bye, *khatam*, finish. That's the story of the decline of the bloody Mughals, I say. All their enemies had bloody *tattoos* which went kitapit kitapit kitapit kitapit faster than they could think. So Aurangzeb the bugger just gave up the chase and said bloody *jané do yaar*. And that, ma boys, is how the Mughal empire ended. You buggers can flesh out all the precise historical details in your homework books. I've given you the skeleton, you give me the flesh. Now it's time for some questions. Aurangzeb the bugger's biggest problem was, do you know who?'

'Sir sir sir sir sir sir sir sir.'

Three hands were up in the air. The brighter boys always waved their hands frantically, wanting to answer the Panther's early questions so as to be just that little bit distant from a beating if they later failed to answer a more difficult question.

The Panther allowed Raj Kumar Kripal to answer.

'Transport, sir.'

A hysterical giggle was suppressed into a quickly vanishing grin by my brother. Kripal's answer was logical enough as a sequel to the Panther's account of Mughal decline, but everyone knew immediately it was the wrong answer simply because the Panther didn't look amused. Or perhaps it was the right answer; it was merely not the answer the Panther had in mind.

'Heh heh heh, bloody transport eh? Come here men. *Hamara nageechoo bloody ao.* Always in a bloody hurry to answer questions ya bugger? You think transport is a *who*? Bloody transport eh? Next time listen carefully to the question.'

One sadistic, stinging blow later, R.K. Kripal was a red-faced boy on his chair; there were no waving hands in the air.

'You ya bugger de Rozio, useless worthless bugger I say. If you can't get me port I hope you can at least tell me who was Aurangzeb the bugger's biggest problem, heh heh heh.'

The Panther was on the prowl for his next victim, and we knew de Rozio was in for it. My brother recollected the current of common apprehension that flowed through everyone in the class that day, bonding them within a petrified silence through the agony of the passing seconds that lay between de Rozio and the Panther's powerful hands. This was a feeling with which everyone in the class was familiar. It happened regularly; in our school we were resigned to the fact that history repeated itself in this way and that no one could ever escape it. De Rozio had never been one of the hand-waving boys who succeeded in answering the

Panther's questions. Aurangzeb had obviously had problems with his weighed-down war-horse, but it seemed reasonably clear that the right answer for the end of empire wasn't the name of that horse. My brother didn't know who else had plagued Aurangzeb, nor did anyone else in the class. Aurangzeb was likely to have had several dozen enemies up his sleeve, and it seemed, on balance, more dangerous to try your luck with a name than to just lie low. The thing to do was to look humble, mentally prepare your skin for pain, try and calm your racing mind, and cling with desperation to the knowledge that the present would fade into a past, taking history and the Panther away with it.

But de Rozio didn't seem to be doing any of these things. He seemed in possession of some peculiar knowledge which gave him the power to look with defiant clarity at the Panther. It made my brother's class frightened and uncomfortable and unsettled. History was not following its expected course and my brother's mind, Richter-scaled to register even the silences that preceded seismic echoes, tried desperately to stem the tremors that gathered like waves towards an apocalypse.

But the age of miracles had not passed. My brother recalled the incredible collective astonishment of everyone in the class when de Rozio, against every odd, came out with the answer which was in the Panther's mind.

'Shivaji the Maratha,' said de Rozio.

My brother remembered the precise clarity and the exact tone of voice with which de Rozio said those words, just as, sitting by the Pangong Lake, he remembered de Rozio's strange remark that the lake looked like it was all made of blazer cloth. He remembered de Rozio saying 'Shivaji the Maratha' without adding the customary 'sir' at the end of that incredible piece of correct information. The precision with which de Rozio uttered those three words and the careful absence of the vital honorific at the end of them made him sound grown-up; almost, said my brother, as though de Rozio thought he was Shivaji himself, facing Aurangzeb the Mughal Emperor as an equal.

It was clear from the moment's silence that followed de Rozio's answer, and from the Panther's infuriated scowl, that his victim had scrambled up a tree he couldn't climb. He would have to ask another question which would bring de Rozio down and within reach. We all knew this; we knew that it would happen; it was, for us, the lesson of history. Until that day de Rozio had offered not the remotest indication of possessing the enormous conceptual resources required to cut loose from the vice-like hegemony in which our lives were held for almost all our years in that school. Dissent was unthinkable, and even by the Pangong Lake, so many years later, my brother was unable to fully account for the way in which de Rozio so simply turned the tables on the Panther, and his own mental world upside down.

De Rozio did not wait for the next question. He knew it would be beyond his ken and that it would make him, in some sense, legitimately accessible to the Panther. He got up from his chair and my brother saw him walk in a determined way straight up to the desk behind which the Panther sat. Then, he said – and this was something we always found both difficult to believe and wonderful to hear – then, he said, he saw de Rozio pick up the cane which lay on the Panther's desk. He saw de Rozio pick up the cane and he saw the swift, stinging, whip-like movement with which de Rozio brought the cane crashing down upon the Panther's pencil moustache and teeth. My brother saw the Panther's dark pencil moustache crumple and twist into blood, and he saw the reflex movement of the Panther's hands as they rushed to rescue his mouth. He saw de Rozio run out of the class but remembered the ensuing pandemonium only dimly because after this his mind went blank with the event. Someone ran out in the direction in which de Rozio had gone, others pelted frantically towards the principal's office, some helped the Panther limp into the infirmary. De Rozio was caught hiding by the ox-bow lake and shut into a high room until the principal, as bewildered as the rest of the school, had measured out meet punishment for a crime that defied conception. The period bell rang out indifferently, signalling the end of that period of history. Everyone was aghast with excitement and awaited the next momentous event – a public thrashing, disgrace, expulsion, something only fractionally short of a grotesque and mangled death. But all this was never to be; that night de Rozio made his escape down a rusting drainpipe and disappeared forever from the school, leaving my brother with the complicated business of rearranging his whole way of thinking about life.

Although he did not see de Rozio after he escaped our school, an image of de Rozio stayed dormant in my brother's mind and he never ceased wondering what happened to him. I think de Rozio became for my brother a concept he could chase in several directions within his own mind. What *really* became of de Rozio didn't bother him terribly; de Rozio was never in the news, nor became the chief minister of Goa, nor, like many of the people of his community, did he ever become Robert the Second Sidekick to Jaykay the Archvillain in every Hindi movie. He was not to be found playing 'Come September' on the electric guitar, wearing drainpipes and an oily Elvis Presley puff in the Royal Café band, nor 'Oh Bloody Oh Bloodah' in the sleazier cafés by the sluggish river where men with silver rings on all their fingers and one long painted red nail drank Black Knights and lurched in surreptitious Fiats towards their uncertain nightly orgasms. He was never seen by my brother in all the private schools he visited for three years as a travelling salesman, persuading impecunious and corrupted schoolteachers to prescribe the books his organization published, wondering if one day he might hear news of the long-vanished de Rozio, or see him suddenly as the inevitable schoolteacher saying, 'Men Men C'mon Men,' his pink acne guarded by sideburns or a stubble, his familiar black drainpipes and pointed black Bata shoes complemented now by a slackening necktie and a thickening chin. He was never a roadside mechanic affably guarding from his customers a mind fine-tuned to the exact degree they could be overcharged, nor was he ever any of those that screamed for a spanner or a screwdriver at emaciated and blackened little boys who washed motorcycle carburettors with old sarees and the darkening petrol that dripped from their hands into the rusting hub-caps of Ambassadors. Vincente de Rozio disappeared into a silence as profound as the one that lay over the Pangong Lake, an aesthetic oblivion, and to my brother it did not really matter, beyond the immense curiosity of his imagination, that he was never able to find him and place him and fix him to one particular spot. What *really* happened to Vincente de Rozio after he ran away from the school seemed almost, in retrospect, a tiresome question. It was the sort of question asked by empiricist historians, or by people systematically conditioned to seek a banal satisfaction in the meaninglessness of ordinary events, never in the imaginative construction of possible stories and multiple endings that might prove more interesting, much more real, and infinitely more wonderful on account of their remoteness from the predictability of objective truths. But this valorization of fiction, this boredom with the truth, it turned out, also had its ironic aspect, for when I think about what *really* happened to my brother in connection with de Rozio, it seems to me that the truth can occasionally be more satisfying than fiction.

After he quit his job as a travelling salesman of textbooks, my brother wandered off to make love to Scandinavian women and look at fjords in Norway. That done, he left for the lochs of Scotland, and, having trekked through the Highlands towards Loch Lomond, he reached Glasgow. Here he stayed with a Sindhi chemist called Bhagwan Brahmani who manufactured test-tube babies.

My brother told me later how test-tube babies were done, and it sounded quite simple really, just like many of the other things that make up life. The Sindhi chemist would take an egg, extracted by a gynaecologist from the insides of a woman. He would put this egg into a special soup which kept it fresh and preserved. Next, he would take a phial of frozen sperm from his deep-freeze, unfreeze it, and empty its contents into the soup. Millions of sperm would immediately begin thrashing each other and their tails in a frantic clamber to mate with the egg. My brother saw them all through a microscope, swimming desperately within their soup, a purple-coloured lake, towards an island which falsely beckoned as refuge. None of them seemed to know or care that they were all doomed, except for one. The egg towards which they were flagellating themselves was physiologically monogamous. It protected itself from multiple entry by a circular ring which allowed only one sperm to break through into its nucleic paradise. The very moment of life at which that one lucky sperm made it across the lake was the exact moment of death for the million others who, oblivious of their destiny, continued in helpless, restive travel to the end. The egg was Shabana Azmi, said my brother, the sperms thrashing about looked like the rest of the world swimming to its doom upon the Pangong Lake.

It seems the Glasgow clinic in which this Bhagwan Brahmani made his test-tube babies was flooded with customers from the Orient. Women came to it from the Middle East, where they were hungry for sperm that would make them socially productive, and from the Indian subcontinent, where rich Hindu women in Hawaii slippers and nylon-georgette sarees searched for the sperm of tall, fair-skinned vegetarian Hindus, caste no bar. My brother's chemist friend bought and sold sperm by the gram, for it was in demand in many of the test-tube baby clinics of the West and fetched a reasonable living. Being of Indian origin, and with the success of Sindhi enterprise in his genes, he'd decided to specialize in Third World sperm, and this had paid off. His sperm bank was a deep-freeze full of phials. He showed these to my brother, rubbing his paunch.

My brother, as I said, got on well with all sorts of people. They showed him the most odd and amazing things in all the different parts of the world where he travelled. This paunch-rubbing crotch-scratching Sindhi chemist, for instance, who made his living by freezing and unfreezing the stuff of life – I doubt that he would have let *me* into his world in the casual and disarming way in which he let in my brother. People never needed to be guarded or defensive or closed up with my brother; he was a traveller, and this was an aura within his personality that Sindhi businessmen too could sense. They knew he wasn't ever going to compete with them, that he would move on and look at other things, that his interest in their world lacked purpose in their sense of that word.

And so my brother saw Bhagwan Brahmani's fridgeful of tubes, with several billion possible lives frozen inside, all awaiting a solution. One tube was labelled: 'Sunni Muslim, non-vegetarian, brown skin, hair curly black, 5ft 8in'; another read: 'Hindu, vegetarian, fair skin, hair straight, 5ft 10in'; and so on. The sperm donors had to be at least 5 feet 8 inches tall and capable of a thick ejaculation, else the creative potential within the fluid fell below the desired level and the sperm count was too low for it to be commercially viable. It wouldn't do if you were short, because women almost invariably wanted tall offspring. Brahmani's phials were mainly full of potential Hindus, Muslims, Buddhists, and Sikhs, but his collection was also known for its variety and elaborate subdivisions. He'd collected fluid from Hindu Jats, Haryanvi Sikhs, Bengali Muslims, Syrian Christian Keralites and Telugu Brahmins. One of the numerous greatgrandsons of Mahatma Gandhi – medical ethics forbade him saying which – had filled one of his phials, and my brother saw this tube, a billion possible Gandhis awaiting their thaw within a purple solution. There were also three test-tubes called Tamil Tigers; Bhagwan Brahmani said these were part of his belief in forward trading, an investment in a future when women from Sri Lanka started coming into money and ran short of men.

The going rate for ten grammes of sperm was quite a lot in those early days, when people were always mildly inhibited or embarrassed or alarmed at being asked to spout into a phial. My brother merely needed the fifty pounds on offer and was amused at the thought of his fluid travelling pell-mell over a purple lake to fulfil the needs of unknown women. A couplet from Dryden floated in and floated out, when man on many multiplied his kind, ere one to one was cursedly confined. The chemist showed him into a room plastered with posters of women in the nude, posing seductively to tease out the desired flow. An Air India calendar made up of Mughal miniature paintings hung incongruously amid the posters: it said March 1988, but the picture on it was not calculated to arouse. It showed what looked like a Mughal court scene, with the Emperor Aurangzeb gazing at his retinue of courtiers, and then helplessly beyond that towards the succulent delights on offer upon the next poster. My brother thought back to Aurangzeb and the rebellions of Vincente de Rozio and Shivaji the Maratha as he slowly felt himself coming to the end of the Mughals in a mix of memory and desire.

As he put my brother's tube into his freezer, Bhagwan Brahmani said it looked rich enough for ten women. 'Ideal for Goans, Anglo-Indians and fairer-skinned subcontinentals generally,' he said with a satisfied look at the colloid. 'Many of them aren't fussy about its religious composition if I tell them it's unusually potent,' he said. At a hundred pounds a head, he winked, he was going to make a killing in the market.

The Zoji La, a mountain pass which leads from Kashmir into Ladakh, usually thaws to the annual flow of traffic and travel in July. A day's hard drive takes the traveller to Kargil, halfway to Leh. Another nine hours through spectacular but infertile terrain dominated by the ascetic heights of Buddhist monasteries ends by the pale blue flow of the Indus at Leh. My brother crossed Zoji La in the August of 1989. He was heading for the Pangong Lake, so he did not stop for long in Leh. He passed Tankse on his way and remembered it as a familiar name, connecting it with de Rozio only five hours later, by the lake. He sat upon the garnet stones near the lake all through that afternoon, until a yak disappeared entirely into a cream-coloured hill. Then he made his way back to Tankse, where he hoped to scrounge out a night's halt in an army barrack.

Four army officers stood talking in a group, and my brother, ever anxious to establish contact with people who might command and bestow shelter, stopped his motorcycle by them. Introducing himself, he asked if he could hole out for the night in one of their encampments. One of the officers looked at him intently and seemed to listen carefully to his voice.

'Aren't you from my school?' he asked finally, after a few sentences of conversation.

'Yes,' said my brother slowly, seeing the marks of acne on the man's face and sifting urgently through his mental files.

'Vincente de Rozio's the name,' he heard the man say. 'Remember me?'

My brother said Vincente and he caught up with each other that night and exchanged their life histories, from the time de Rozio fled the school to the time his own regiment, like his father's, got posted to Tankse, near the Pangong Lake. It seems nothing very spectacular ever happened to de Rozio after he got away from the school. I think my brother found this fairly disappointing, having stored him up in his mind as a symbol of the most consummate and successful rebellion he'd ever experienced. But we believed in fiction, and things that seemed disappointing about real-life characters didn't bother us excessively, because we knew there was always more to people than met the eye. And as it turned out my brother was able, in the end, to retain his image of de Rozio as a character whose life was tied by some strange destiny to his own.

De Rozio told my brother he'd run off to railway relatives and finished school privately, then joined the army, and now spent most of his time skiing and playing golf. My brother saw no sign of the extraordinary in his eyes; a Spartacus once, he seemed now to have become like the rest of us, a father and a friend. He had married five years earlier and said with predictable, commonplace pride that he had a daughter; she was just over a year old. 'Must tell you the extraordinary way in which we got her, men,' he added.

144

There was no stopping people once they started confiding in my brother. The travel aura around him said very clearly he wasn't competing, that he could be trusted with things that were intimate and needed guarding against other people, that he would be moving on to look at other things. It made the women let their hair down and open up with him in ways they just wouldn't with me. It made de Rozio comfortable and relaxed enough to want to part with something personal, almost as though he needed to share something that belonged only to him with my brother.

'To tell you the truth,' he said, a minute or so before my brother left that part of the world, 'she's not my daughter at all, strictly speaking, but just keep this to yourself, men. Thing is we tried for three years to get a child but it just wouldn't work, y'know. Anyway, an old pal of mine in the II Sikh Rifles suggested this place called Third World Clinic in Scotland, and so off we went to one of these sperm merchant fellahs they have there, some Sindhi chappie called Brahmani or something li' that. I say, men, these Sindhis will sell you just about anything.'

He laughed, and my brother forced out a smile. 'Anyway,' said Vincente, 'long and short of it is that now we have a bonny little lass. Must show you her picture some day.'

My brother swung to the correct position on his motorcycle, flexing himself to begin the next leg of his travels.

He felt the cold air of Ladakh on his hands.

He saw his past swim volitionless over purple-blue water into a future de Rozio, and, as he adjusted his dark glasses, the colour of the Pangong Lake came into his eyes.

'Yes,' he said vacantly. 'Yes, you really must,' he said.

A Passage through India

When I looked at my brother in his late thirties I saw a middle-aged Zeus, fading towards Beethoven and misplaced upon the urban sprawl of north India, with a porous identity embedded in him like layers of the earth. Superficially, he was an international traveller in whom our country lay skin deep: its sun had vaguely coloured his epidermis and its landscapes had shaped his rugged features with aesthetic imprecision, so that if you parachuted him anywhere along the line of latitude which runs midway between the Tropic of Cancer and the Arctic Circle – into the regions of Sparta or Granada or Shiraz or Tashkent or Samarkand – the native women who were certain to come running up would take him in as a good-looking god who fell to them with no strings attached. But I could see deeper than that: for all his travels, his physiognomy was firmly anchored in India. The country's shorelines had deepened his face and hands, its mountains had sunk into his mind, and the regularity of its weather pattern had come to determine his moods and inner certainties. India's boundaries contained friends, monuments, feelings, fragrances, saleable commodities and all the multiple rustles of a currency which made no sense in dollars.

This was an obscure feeling. It lay in my brother like a dormant volcano because, like upheavals of the earth, music and the odd book had piratically cut his moorings from our shores and taken the *Hispaniola* of his mind to the envapoured silver caskets of many treasure islands, where the demarcated flow of rivers was flooded to a single, seismic confluence. Here there was Kubla Khan chaos. The Styx, the Ganga, the Avon, the Volga, the blue Danube and sundry tributary melodies emerged or disappeared at will in the caverns of his grey cosmos. My brother's innermost travels were the movements of concertos, ragas and symphonies, or the dreams and fantasies of his own creation. They were the asylums of his soul, the pulsations of his heart against passport officials and the temple cacophony of our country's nationalist rhetoric. It was much the same with me, really, though when I looked in the mirror I knew that if I descended upon the women of Shiraz or Tashkent, their expressions would be less hospitable.

A more fundamental difference between us was the way we listened to music, and it is in part on account of this difference that I no longer listen to the 'Emperor' Concerto with the relaxed intensity I once did. That music sets up a revolution in my mind and dredges up associations and images, particularly of my brother's unkempt-composer look, his dishevelled hair, his wild-calm eyes and hooded Spartan austerity, images which haunt me towards a restiveness I can no longer bear.

They would not have haunted my brother. In his mind, music was a reprieve from images. He disliked knowing the stories of operas because their absurd heroics and sentimentality seemed to pull them down into a universe of idiotic and unpoetic words, while their melodies strained another way, freeing them from earthly connection and giving them transcendent sense. It was not that way for me: I was engaged in a fruitless quest for exact meanings. When I listened to music, my mind was sorting out its structure. When he listened to music, my brother's eyes were shut and his mind undone. His listening was *purer* than mine, if that is the word: at least, since it was free of real-life impressions, I assume it was somehow more *essential* and closer to the heart of sound. The 'Emperor' Concerto swam into his mind like a continent, an amorphous and unfixed universe of no specific borders, a song of vast spaces which carried no associations that could pull him down into the demarcated areas of daily living. But I, the lesser vehicle, am constrained by the thoughts which come into my head when that music plays. It reminds me of the dreams we shared, and of the way my brother looked on the day we finally went to see the Taj Mahal in Agra.

I remember precisely when we first resolved to see the Taj. It was when the Golden Temple of Amritsar was stormed by the Indian army and nearly flushed out of existence along with the Sikh separatists who had made that temple their fortress. When this happened, my brother and I were jolted out of our nearly lifelong slumber in worlds far removed from our country. At that time he was travelling mentally through Scandinavia, listening to the music of Sibelius and watching the films of Ingmar Bergman. I was drifting soulfully through intergalactic time, reading Milan Kundera and formulating cross-cultural aphorisms: a dog, I told myself, might be defined by Kundera as an animal which likes being stroked without becoming possessive or traumatized. I looked in the mirror and felt like a Golden Retriever. I stuck out my tongue and panted hard. Then I quit fooling because I saw that my eyes had gone gentle with age. In those days, before the Temple was invaded, I felt like a satellite. I was one with the cosmos. When I reached up I felt the womblike warmth of an Indian sky. Only the Buddha had fewer possessions and more salvation than I. Then, suddenly, the air got so thickly clouded with the bullets fired by politics into religion that my brother and I both went into a spin and had to bale out of our solipsisms. We crashlanded back home with fractured minds.

Subcontinental aircrashes, even when conceptual, are not free of the slush of politics, and I could trace the causes of the Temple's destruction and our mental nosedive back into India from the unhedged terrains of our mind to an earlier time, to the slow erosion of Mahatma Gandhi's spirit by cobra politicians, to the dispersal of Nehru's misty and avuncular sanity by Indira Gandhi and the venomous snakepit of new leaders which she spawned, to the KGB's octopus tentacles and the CIA's foreign hand. Perhaps nothing short of a Tristram Shandyian ramble which fleshed out our souls within the social and political history of our country, and perhaps not even that, would breathe life into that period of our lives: so the Golden Temple only serves as a starting point of sufficient lustre, because when it got punctured to a pincushion by slow-motion boomerang bullets which tore through it (they reached the body of Indira Gandhi some months later) my brother and I realized, living in India, how far we were from our own country.

'Listen,' I said to him, looking at newspaper pictures of that devastated monument, 'd'you realize we haven't even seen the Taj Mahal? We better go and see it someday soon, before that gets cordoned off too, or taken over, or pulled down. This is India.'

'The Taj? Who's fighting over that? It's outside politics. Don't get paranoid.'

I thought of our parents, who had concluded their honeymoon with a photograph taken on the marble bench which floats in front of the Taj, and who would not have used the word paranoid. In their generation people were merely nervous. I saw Abba in a fading black-and-white photo, wearing a pin-stripe suit and a precarious smile. He had lost his voice on their wedding day and croaked his way through their honeymoon. Amma was beaming quietly inwards and looked as though she had words enough for them both. She wore a 1950s bun done up with two-pronged pins which jutted out of her hair like little antennae.

In my mind I saw the settled sepia of the way they looked. It contrasted vividly with the hedonistic colour of our lives. The pictures of their days together are still held in place by ornate stick-down corners in black paper albums which have delicate white interleaved sheets. Everything is firmly in position, all in black and white, the natural colours of their time. Those pictures show me people who had a clear relationship with each other, with their beliefs, with their values, with their monuments, with their town, with their country, with the overarching sky. They suggest a clarity which my brother and I seemed to have lost in a world overdosed now by garishnesss, now by subtle shades and tones. The photographs were taken by a Baby Brownie box in the simple era which came before people had to focus first on their camera, fit the right lens, choose between manual and automatic, check the shutter speed, shoot the object in front and move quickly to the next kill.

The Taj comes out best in the earlier pictures, clear, solid, calmly symbolic. Looking at my parents' photos I wondered if either of us would have felt Indian enough to conclude our honeymoon with a secular pilgrimage to the country's aesthetic centrepoint. I doubted it. If my brother or I had married at all, we would most likely have followed some simple ceremony with a journey to the Pangong Lake, to the enormous tranquillity of a landscape in which we could be oblivious of India, a region uncontaminated by politicians and crowds where the shadow lines of our country merged with those of Tibet and China into navy-blue water and an aquamarine sky, a vista devoid of the black-and-white clarity with which the Taj had seemed to epitomize India.

But on that day it was perhaps the unease I felt at the fragility of all our relationships, specially with our country, which made my voice resolute. 'You've studied history,' I said. 'Nothing's permanent. I think we should go and see the Taj.'

My brother looked up sharply and didn't speak for a bit. 'I guess that's so,' he admitted finally. 'Yes, okay, let's go and see the damn thing. Maybe the politicians will break that down too, though I can't see how.'

I couldn't see how either, but I knew inside myself that I didn't possess the certainties of the old world. All around me the air was crackling with pious loudspeaker speeches about holy cows, but there were no real holy cows, only cows that foraged for plastic and paper who were opportunely decked up and paraded for money in the regalia of religion. All around me there were men with paunches called property developers choking the cities for cash which they shared with national politicians and international bankers. All around me there were crumbling walls and shaky monuments which had once seemed like the Rock of Gibraltar. It wasn't even all that clear to me, in the way I suppose it had been to my parents, that the Taj was quintessentially Indian. Was the 'Emperor' Concerto quintessentially German? Were Sibelius and Bergman indubitably Scandinavian? If the Alhambra were put on the banks of the Yamuna and the Taj repositioned upon the low hills of Granada would it make much difference or either less beautiful? If we learnt Mughal history in English and dreamt in Hindi about Elizabeth Taylor did it diminish our vision of the Taj? Would they inherit the Indian earth who saw the Taj as a national monument, or would the manna of heaven fall to those who described it as a medieval Muslim structure? I was beseiged by a universe of questions in which there were no straight answers, and the overarching sky, once powered by deities and the monsoon rain, was now showering down a confusion of radio signals.

My mind switched from one thing to another as rapidly as television channels and I recalled the Bengali American professor of deconstruction I had once loved, my very own Tiresian s/he, who had started off male, sex-changed to womanhood, and finally regained the apparatus of masculinity. She had opened my eyes to the flexibility, the changeability, the instability of all identities. It confirmed what I had learnt from the Bible, where it says that skin can be made to stretch more than rubber, for didn't Jesus tie his ass to a tree and walk a mile? How much easier, then, for Gorbachev to break up Russia and the Berlin Wall, and for me to see India crack up like the fragments of my multi-channelled mind.

All this got me wondering gloomily if my anxiety to see the Taj was only a desperate effort to assert some simple notion of India into a crumbling picture of our country. Whatever the truth, and never mind if there was none, whatever the real reason, and never mind if it was illogical, I felt quite clearly that it was urgent now for us to see the Taj, and also vaguely that we were guilty of not even having made an effort to see what might prove a visual equivalent of the 'Emperor' Concerto.

Having resolved to go, we should of course have gone

immediately. My parents, in such a situation, would have dispatched a minion to the railway station for tickets. Indecision was not among Amma's afflictions. English literature had provided her with many clear morals. She was doubly guarded against the dangers of procrastination by her close examination of *Hamlet* and 'The Love Song of J. Alfred Prufrock'. Overnight, she and Abba would have grasped the Mughal bounties of Agra and come back secure, fulfilled, satisfied, all unease quelled. That, at least, was how I saw them. But then I wondered if they were differently constituted, or if the disquietude they must have experienced at times was merely less visible to me. One could speculate endlessly. I gave up. Beyond intelligent guesses there seemed no way of knowing what really happened inside other people.

Yet the differences between them and us were clear enough: my brother and I made no concrete move to reach Agra. The Taj disappeared from our heads with the Golden Temple and for short bursts of time we managed to disappear back into music and the serenity of our Golden Retriever minds.

But as the days passed, my discomfort with the way I was and the way things were began to eat into me. The passage of time seemed to possess a different quality now. The newspapers carried political crises every day and the country lurched like a zombie into a future blinkered by mindless notions of the past. Our musical refuge from what other people called reality began to seem frailer and less serene, and our tenuous relationship with the unreal country outside made my blood course with the hormones of apocalypse. I felt bloated with the violence of a battered world, with feelings far exceeding the unease I had felt when Nehru died. Was I Indian? Was I Indian enough? What did being Indian mean? I felt I was Indian, but I wasn't clear how. I saw our remoteness from things that were Indian in other people's minds, and yet I couldn't escape feeling Indian. It seemed almost a genetic compulsion to feel Indian, and over the next few months as the intermezzo of our inner travels was interrupted with the regularity of a heartbeat by a trinity of scoundrels, politicians and godmen, as a prime minister was killed, Sikhs murdered, Muslims and Christians made fearful, and as everyone searched for where they belonged, for what belonged to them, and whether anything belonged to anyone for any length of time, I wanted more and more to see the Taj. In my mind I saw it stand wanly in the distance, its solidity discoloured by a sudden frailty. There was a gnawing anxiety about it in my mind.

But the urgency of reaching the Taj only came to a head when politics once again tore venomously into religion and we found ourselves looking at pictures of another ruined monument. This time it was the Babri Masjid, a mosque which had stood so harmlessly through the centuries that people didn't even know it was there. Then the politicians twisted it out of obscurity and began dressing it up with holiness like a cow till fanatics in saffron pulled it down with tridents. Soon they were spreading like locusts towards other monuments. This time there was no space for words. 'Listen,' I said, 'I'm getting us tickets for Agra.'

I took a tonga to the railway station for the tickets. The horse was dead and covered in flies. The tongawallah flogged him back to life and he lurched into a zombie's canter. The flies flew off to inhabit another dead country one horse away.

There was a flurry of things to think about through the metronomic clatter of time's winged chariot. The streets which had once passed me by in a blur seemed thick and sharp with crowds which wove themselves into my mind. As we moved from the domain of large houses, through the infinite anonymity of housing colonies, past the shrunken spread of slums, a lifetime of solipsism slipped behind and the bungalows of our minds, in which my brother and I had lived for long, seemed to crumble like broken monuments. I felt as vulnerable as a half-dead horse.

Tickets were readily available for the next night; it was the worst of times, there was the memory of recent riots, and people were not venturing out unless they had to. I woke next morning to the sound of the 'Emperor' Concerto, with which it made sense to start the superhuman endeavours of each new day, and in the evening, when we took a tonga to the railway station, I remember my brother's abstract-troubled look. It was a new look, and I saw from it that the unmapped continent of music in his head had been untuned by the discord of a counterfeit country. When I looked in the mirror, I saw in it the image of my brother. The Golden Retriever had gone.

The overnight train between our city and Agra is the most convenient way of travelling between those two junctions – I might even say the happiest. Unlike trains which snake in late to clamorous platforms, the Agra Mail comes from nowhere and is always waiting when you reach the station. At one end the smoke hisses peacefully from its head, as though from some gentle dragon digesting a heavy meal. At the other end a red flag guards a tail, keeping the beast in patient slumber. You climb into your compartment just after dinner, spread a sheet over a reserved berth, assess the culture and income of your neighbours, read a book until dinner is digested, and fall asleep dreaming of the Taj Mahal.

The train slips gently into the night. Its wheels clatter to a monotonous tune which seems carefully calculated to match the regularity of a sleeper's heartbeat. Four times the train halts for breath, regains steam, and starts again with the determination of a long-distance runner. Its stops are brief. They serve as respites which allow its long intestine of passengers to turn in their sleep without fear of falling. The train is seldom late. In the early morning you can buy earth-coloured tea in rustic cups of baked clay. When I was young, station tea was always sickly sweet. But over the years, as the price of sugar has risen, its contamination of platform beverages has fallen to a pleasant level.

After tea the wheels of the train change their sounds to the wakeful rhythms of a new day. They clash and shudder against fishplates as the single stem-line of night blossoms into a day's flower of railway lines. The mist of dawn clears over Agra, holding the promise of marble monuments. As the train sidles along a tarmac, you feel within reach of Mughal splendour.

On a February night, nearly thirty years after Nehru's death and a couple of months after the clearing out of his spirit from the country, I saw the Agra Mail waiting to take us on our first visit to the Taj. I remembered the day that Nehru had died, ruining our colony cricket match, and I imagined I saw neighbourhood cows cross a railway track on which a man pissed in the far distance. Another man winched up the parallel bars of a railway gate, and I watched as those bars changed in my mind from the twin cerulean rockets of childhood to iron rods of demarcation.

I hoped the train would run on time. We climbed cleanly through a hatch which led into its neat metallic entrails: we had not fought the world to get a berth. I had reserved our places as efficiently as my mother.

We sat down and began our ritual assessment of fellow travellers: a lady gracefully greying with the languid eyes of an ageing Labrador, no husband in sight, English-speaking Bengali by the looks of her saree, handwriting probably rounded neat as a Loretto nun, unlikely to snore. Next to her a definite snorer, a borrower of other men's newspapers, a slurper of tea, a belcher with many active orifices who seemed capable of incredible things at night. Some distance from him a youngish woman who looked a Keralite. She had been speaking to the older lady and didn't seem connected to the man. Perhaps a trained nurse from the south who had found work in a hospital up north.

There were four berths. If one of the other three people in front of us didn't disembark soon, there would be five claimants for four berths. I hoped the fat man would leave.

It is customary to establish a close relationship with one's immediate neighbours in a bogey, so that by the time the journey is done the chances are good that you will marry the daughter of the man with whom you have travelled, or at least gain a sister for a few hours if the person on the next berth seems single and a woman. But that night, though there was a potential nurse at

155

hand, neither of those things seemed a possibility. The young Keralite looked rather closed up, the other lady looked too old, and the man was so pot-bellied and full of oil that I wouldn't have married his daughter even if she had danced like a houri from the Bosphorus. My mind switched instantaneously to a limerick.

> Twin houris of the Bosphorus
> Had eyes that shone like phosphorus.
>> The sultan cried 'Troth!
>> I will marry you both!'
> But they said 'No, you'll have to toss for us.'

An enviable situation. I looked dolefully at the two women in front. On every side of us there were screaming infants. Their tired mothers soothed them with thumps, ignoring other children who scampered up and down the aisle with the joyful frenzy of the very young.

The greasepot, whose first instinct was to scratch his lower half, looked at us. 'You are going to Agra?'

We nodded. So did the Loretto Labrador. The younger woman didn't say anything.

'I am going to the ticket collector to check my ticket. My luggage is here. Just now I will be back. Until then you can kindly . . .'

We nodded our assent, and as he left a child came flying through the air and crashed straight into my midriff. I over-balanced and fell backwards, more or less directly into the lap of the next-berth lady – the older one, as luck would have it. The child rocketed off with a yelp in the direction of other midriffs, leaving me with a close relationship.

'I er . . . these children, ah, I mean, I hope you . . .'

'It's OK, really, I'm OK, er . . .'

'You are, I mean, you are also going to Agra?' After such prox-imity, I hoped I sounded vaguely sane. I saw a half-smile play about my brother's lips. The lady's saree was white with a red border and there was a faint virginal dent at the point where our bodies had met.

'Oh yes.' She smiled politely.

I turned to the younger woman, trying to draw her in. 'How about you?'

'Oh yes,' she said, but looked away, retreating into herself. Perhaps she too was far from her roots and wanted to be left alone.

The older lady seemed to feel she ought to compensate for the younger woman's withdrawal. 'And you?' she asked. 'Are you going up to Agra?'

'Yes, first time.'

'Oh, then you have never seen . . .'

'No, we haven't, neither my brother nor I.' (They smiled an introduction at each other.) 'We have been planning to see it for a long time, but it's always got postponed. Then just when all this trouble started we finally got around to it.'

'Oh is that so?' she said. 'It's strange, isn't it, how things get postponed. It's the same with me. Not the Taj, I mean, I've seen that, every day, in fact, when I was young, because there was a view of it from our old house and I could see it from morning to night. But it's true that one takes things for granted and they get postponed and then suddenly you feel you have to do them. I should have sold my house in Agra ages back, and now, just when property values have crashed, I feel I simply must sell it quickly, and these things take such a long time.'

'You have a house with a view of the Taj, and you want to sell it?'

'Oh yes I must, it was a lovely rambling old house and it even had peacocks in the lawn once, they would come in the early mornings and occasionally in the evenings because I always kept food for them to peck at, they're such shy birds, but Agra is no place to live in any more, unless you're there for a short stay to see the sights. At one time it had a nice small-town atmosphere and there was space to breathe and walk, but now it's as congested and polluted as Calcutta without any of the good things in Calcutta, so I've settled there instead.'

'Ah yes, I see,' I said, and oh, so she is a Bong, I thought. Likes living in Calcutta too, like all the rest of them. Probably sings Tagore songs all day long. Bong song, all day long. Bong song, all day long. Soon my mind was a train rattling out the rhythm of a single line.

> Bongsong bongsong, bongsong bongsong.
> Daylong daylong, daylong daylong.

At least she feels at home where she lives, I thought. Bongsong bongsong, daylong daylong. The train's interminable cadence drilled that line into my head. At least she can sing songs in her mother tongue, I thought, bonglong longbong, songlong longsong. I thought about cricket and Nehru and peacocks on a lawn which had once looked to me like mobile beds of blue roses, and suddenly I realized I had never seen a baby peacock. What did baby peacocks look like, I wondered. Were they miniature versions of their parents when they hatched, or did they start off black-and-white and gain colour over the years? I made a mental note to find this out. Then I looked at the old lady and knew she was nice because she made me feel like a dog, like a Pekinese called Iago who has sniffed out something pleasant. I wagged my tail amiably. What she had said made sense. You can usually tell from people's eyes and inflections whether they make sense to you or not, and I could tell from her tone and apparel and general demeanour that her way of thinking was in tune with ours, just as I sensed our distance from our other two neighbours. The girl from Kerala looked nice enough, but in wanting her own space, like the rest of us, she kept all doors firmly shut to preclude the risk of intrusion. It was a feeling I understood. She made me feel like a Jack London Husky, aloof and glad of my own body warmth.

The man looked very different. With him I felt like a Dobermann. When I looked at him I knew my eyes had gone impassive and that my tail was still. He looked straight out of the cow belt, where the Mughals had once set up cultural enclaves and water-channelled tombs alongside their fortifications, and where the architecture of the old world was slowly being swallowed up by the southward spread of Punjab and the musclemen of caste armies. We too had got out of a small town in the cow belt, where a river which once filtered its slow path through the shadows of fading palaces had become the city's sewer, and where swelling crowds were either breaking down the country's old monuments, or living in them, or letting them go to ruin, or ringing them with barbed wire and charging tourists to get through.

'Specially now,' the lady was saying, 'it's not as bad as the Partition in 'forty-seven, but . . .'

The train jerked a little, preparing itself.

'Excuse me, you are on my seat,' said the greasepot suddenly, scowling at my brother.

'I don't think so,' said my brother.

'Kindly check up your place. The train is going to leave. This is my berth,' said the man.

'Kindly check yours,' said my brother, 'this place is mine.'

I ignored the altercation. 'That's true,' I said to the lady, 'once these politicians mobilize the fanatics one just doesn't know what's safe.'

The safari suitor looked apoplectic. 'Kindly show me your ticket,' he said, 'this is my reserved berth.'

He took out a rubber pillow and began puffing up for the night. I wondered where people bought those rubber pillows. Men in safari suits always had blow jobs for train journeys. Perhaps they needed a change from the regular stuff, night after night. Night-night nightnight, nightnight nightnight. The bawling infants had fallen asleep on their mothers.

> Goodnight goodnight, goodnight goodnight.
> Goodnight sweet ladies.
> Goodnight goodnight.

'Yes', said the lady, 'it's almost as bad as those Partition months. Sometimes one really doesn't know what's happening.'

'Or which place is one's own,' said my brother, fishing out his ticket and handing it with studied slowness to the oilcan. 'This place is mine. I think there must be some mistake,' he said.

'Not my mistake, but maybe yours,' retorted the man, examining the ticket with his only non-scratching hand. 'From where did you buy this ticket? This ticket is showing the wrong number. This berth is reserved against my name.'

My brother said nothing. I could see his innards simmer. The air was getting tense. I was beginning to bristle like an Alsatian. 'Let the ticket collector come,' I said, 'he will settle the matter.'

'Yes let him come', said the fellow aggressively. 'We are living in world's largest democracy but I say it is world's largest corruptocracy. In this country for ten lakhs any member of parliament will be ready to commit suicide. Let the ticket-checker come. This berth is mine.'

'Everything's become even more chaotic with these computerized tickets,' said the Bengali lady, trying to ease the air.

'That's true,' my brother said to her, but his voice was directed mostly at the fat man, 'one just doesn't know what's what. You reserve a berth and someone else starts claiming it. You put your money in a bank and they tell you someone else has already taken it out. You look at a mosque one day and the next day they tell you it's a temple. And look at what's happening now. Some people are making it sound as though inside every mosque there's a temple waiting to get out. Three centuries back these same fanatics were pulling down temples and moving in with their mosques, and now we have a new bunch doing the opposite. If one doesn't fight for one's rights someone or the other just moves in and takes over.'

'Good thing they haven't dragged in the churches yet,' I said, wondering if the girl from Kerala would speak up for her faith. But she stayed quite silent, and once again the older woman felt she should keep the flag flying for her sex.

'Yes, it is all quite confusing, I think,' she said. 'It just wasn't like this. You're probably too young to remember Nehru, and maybe he isn't important for young people now, but things were clearer while he was alive, at least for people like me, because *he* was clear about religious tolerance, just like Gandhiji. And look at these politicians now, how they've made everyone so insecure. One has to be so careful about everything nowadays. Look at how just about everything is barricaded these days. They have these endless security checks everywhere. First it was airports, then it was government buildings, and now you have to get through cordons of policemen just to look at the Taj. When I was young there was only a hedge around our house and some gulmohar trees. Then two years ago someone broke in and the police said I should get sentries and a barbed-wire fence. But I don't think *that* stops thieves these days. You can't trust the police, and the courts take years and years so you can't go there either. I just decided it's all too tiring at my age, keeping an old house going from a long distance when I can't really live in it.'

'It must be quite sad, though,' said my brother. 'I think it's a crime to pull down old houses and put up those hideous multi-storeyed blocks, but there's really nothing people like us can do. We're selling out and leaving, or else we're just watching and feeling pretty helpless. Sometimes we burn up with rage and sometimes we make a little noise and go on a march but that doesn't stop things going the way they're going, and they're not going our way, so we just end up living inside our own small enclaves with our own little fortifications. You drop your guard for a minute and someone else clambers in.'

I thought of the unguarded mosque into which people had poured in. It seemed to connect up with the barricaded silence of the nurse opposite. The silence of the hills was being taken over by the clamour of cars. In Musoorie, Manali, Simla, Kodi and Naini Tal a landscape of green and brown trees had turned into the many colours of metal and plastic, and beyond them the glaciers to heaven were paved with the glitter of tin.

'Too many people,' I said.

'Too many fat men,' said my brother. 'Too many fat men taking over other people's spaces. Look what they've done with the Babri Masjid, tomorrow they'll do the same thing in Mathura and Banaras, and then the day after someone will retaliate and pull down a temple, and it'll just go on and on. All our politicians are fat and they all want to get fatter. Have you ever seen a thin politician? Very soon . . .'

The man in the safari suit stopped scratching and butted in with a sneer. 'Masjid? What masjid? Excuse me, that structure is not a mosque. That is just . . .'

'. . . they are taking over other people's places everywhere, these fat people,' continued my brother, looking straight back at him. 'That structure was a mosque till it was pulled down. Maybe it was a temple before that. Before that it was a Buddhist cave for all we know, and before that it might have been a place for animists.'

'Any-miss? What are you talking mister? Do you know any history? Any-miss or any-mister is not my concern,' said the fellow, 'first you kindly check which is your place. This is my seat. And this country is not just for any body. If minorities and pseudo-secularists . . .'

The two women near us were looking worried, specially the younger one.

'Just a minute,' said my brother, realizing that further conversation would only lead to a fracas into which every other male in the bogey would converge, 'there's no point waiting for the ticket collector. The simplest thing is to check the chart.'

'I'll do that,' I said, feeling myself bristle like a guard dog. I told myself to calm down. I changed into a Dachshund and saw myself scurry off to check the chart. The train had given its first hoot and was fidgeting on its wheels. I clawed my way through other necks which craned at the glued-up chart. But the substance with which the printout had been stuck against the outer wall of the train seemed to have eaten through the paper and smudged the area where our names should have been, and it was impossible to ascertain our position inside. There was a Mrs A. Sen who hadn't been swallowed up: Female, Age 58, our Labrador. There was a Ms Susan, Female, Age 29, our sister. But the cow-boy's name wasn't visible on the spot where ours should have been. We would have to await the ticket-checker to resolve our rights. Anyhow, we had valid tickets and could bide our time. I walked back to our berths wondering what Rottweilers looked like.

The train was moving as I got back. 'Nothing is clear,' I said, 'let the ticket-checker come.' Our antagonist muttered and scratched some more and we all waited.

The train gathered speed, flashing past dull suburban tube-lights into a flattened countryside full of lonely trees. Winter had stripped them nearly bare and I saw the extended solitude of their branches. A silence which was like music came into my eyes, and as I watched life go by from the window of that train nothing seemed to matter except the sweep of winter and trees passing. An ecstasy of unfeeling crept into me. There was no past, there was no future, there were no mosques nor caves nor temples, there was just a moon rocking without reason in the sky, showing me the careless downward drift of a leaf or two. I felt dimly grateful for the lunar thoughtlessness of leaves against gravity and for the world of those few fallow moments, laggard of purpose, filled up with casual images, weatherbeaten and floating. It was a going-nowhere world. It gave out a luminous halo which made more sense to me than the metallic universe inside the train, replete with getting-somewhere people, the competent, the ambitious and the gruff-voiced, all ready to conquer the earth at a moment's notice. I was in love with that moon. It was a rocking-chair moon and I, trapped between getting-somewhere people in a train moving with blind determination, fell unreasonably in love with that going-nowhere glow. I remembered my travels with Elizabeth Taylor and Mikhail Gorbachev, I saw Abba afloat on a magic carpet of newspapers and Amma with misty eyes in a fading white saree, and I longed to be the lonely, spaced-out occupant of a skylab which made foredoomed Sisyphean circles like the moon, safe in the knowledge that there was nowhere to get to, pointlessly happy, aimlessly drifting. I saw cows of a vaulting ambition jump over that moon as the lines of an unhurried past came circling motionless into my mind with the inevitability of a satellite whose antennae were bedecked with the orange of gulmohar branches and the yellow of the amaltas:

> I saw a cow
> It was playing with a sow
> And do you know
> Just now
> It jumped over the moon, and how!

And how and how, and how and how, replied the train.

My reverie ended with the ticket-collector's arrival. Our neighbour presented his ticket immediately and began voicing his complaint. Mrs Sen, Ms Susan and the two of us handed over ours, and my brother explained the problem through the loudmouth's plaintive interjections. It took no time to sort it out: my brother's name was on the ticket-checker's chart.

'Your ticket is for tomorrow,' the collector informed our neighbour, whose protestations gave way to angry incoherence against the Union of India and its inefficient railway personnel. The collector was unmoved. 'Your ticket is not valid,' he said. 'You will have to disembark at the next station. Kindly come this way. I will have to see what can be done . . . but it is very difficult . . . let us see . . .'

They went off together, and we knew they would soon come to an understanding; for a small consideration an extra passenger could always be adjusted somewhere in the bogey. Anyhow, we were glad to see the back of him. He returned soon, picked up his suitcase, allowed us to witness one last scratch, and moved on.

Susan and Mrs Sen had lain down already. The train's wheels had accelerated to the placating rhythm of a lullaby. A walkman's earplugs had filled up my brother's ears. I looked out for a while and let the staccato landscape drum itself into my mind. Then I closed my eyes and drifted off.

What a troubled, unsettling dream I had that night. I dreamt I was standing in front of a black-and-white Taj. The pot-bellied man in safari suit was looking at it too, and next to him was the ticket-collector, his villainous little finger entwined in the fat man's index finger. Between them there sat Salvador Dali, who had been commissioned to paint the Taj on his canvas. I peered into the canvas and saw to my horror that the monument he had painted was grotesquely coloured and disproportionate. One half of its dome had the concentric purple folds of an onion, and three of the four minarets which ringed it had collapsed like broken columns among the ruins of ancient Rome. Its platform was a calendar, its months were flapping in the wind, and its dates were falling out of it as tiny parachutes. They looked beautiful, going in all directions, and soon they were spilling out of the canvas and scattering all around me. I tried catching them, but instead I found myself entangled in a floating web of time which set me adrift and put me down after an age upon a black night in a desert of white snow. There was nothing in that desert except the ordered anarchy of snow dunes and snow. I stood there for what seemed like an epoch, unfocussed by the bleakness of that lonely landscape and the blinding anonymity of my own situation within it. I started walking aimlessly to overcome my nauseating fear and a feeling of hopelessness, and then, somewhere in the distance, I heard a familiar tune. The sheer relief of that sound made me weak at the knees and I was flooded with hope, but when I tried whistling that melody to get my bearings on life my breath condensed as tiny white parachutes which fell onto the ground and merged with the snow. I closed my eyes to clear my head, and so I was able to concentrate, and then the music began to make better sense and registered as something I knew and loved. It seemed to me that that music had been playing there forever, waiting to be heard, but my mind had gone so cold that I couldn't make out either where it came from, nor what it meant, nor even what it was called though I racked my dull mind for the names of compositions and composers. Somehow I wanted very badly to discover the exact origin, the exact name, the exact meaning of that music, for I was under the spell of the desperate and hopeless illusion that by knowing such things I would become less lonely, that by the possession of such items of information I would make that music *belong* to me and become part of me *forever*. But before I could concentrate hard enough to make that music mine, it stopped, and instead I saw a huge tidal wave of sound gather to an apocalypse, and then, somewhere in the recesses of my mind, I heard an almighty crash.

As I woke I knew my hands were flying instinctively to save my head from the floor. I managed to stop myself falling off the berth and got up dazed. When my head cleared I realized that the train had come to a very sudden halt and that everyone was gropingly awake. The infants had started up immediately, and people were rushing out to see what had happened. Mrs Sen and Susan were up too, and my brother and I left them sitting near our luggage as we put on our shoes and clutched our way through the compartment's narrow aisle to check what was afoot.

It was a cold night outside. No women had disembarked. The business of ascertaining facts about the functioning world was the exclusive function of the entire country's male population. There were hordes of men along the track, spitting, pissing, scratching, staring with dedication, or just striding up and down in order to feel like Genghis Khan.

'There is an unidentified object on the track,' said one of them, coming up. 'The driver and guard are investigating.'

'Must be a bomb,' said someone else. 'These days terrorists are everywhere. They are getting professional training in Pakistan to blow up Kashmir and Punjab, and now they are gunning for the rest of India.'

Anti-national elements, I thought. All the country's newspapers had taken to running a column every day with the heading:

COPS NAB ANTI-NATIONAL ELEMENTS

Below this the only daily variation was the number of cops involved in the nabbing operation, the number of anti-national elements they had nabbed, and the name of the locality where the above-mentioned anti-national elements had been nabbed. On days when no anti-national elements had been nabbed, the newspapers substituted 'national' with 'social' to denote hoodlums. It provided the entire country with psychological satisfaction to know for a fact, each morning, that villains were being apprehended on a daily basis.

I spotted our ex-neighbour in the distance. There goes a walking, talking anti-national element who hasn't been nabbed, I thought. One day he would be prime minister of the country. At that moment he was walking towards the engine. He certainly has a ticket for the future, I thought, suddenly remembering phrases from Mr Arren's sermon the day that Nehru died: 'I felt lonely and homeless, India seemed a strange and bewildering land, the spectre of religion . . .' A voice brought me back again.

'If the bomb disposal squad has to be summoned we will reach Agra sometime next month,' said someone. His neighbour immediately felt an acute loss of power. 'Next month?' he said with an all-knowing laugh. 'My dear, we will be lucky to reach by next year.' I considered outdoing them both by laughing even louder and saying, 'Next year? My dear, we will be lucky to reach by next century,' but I didn't. They both looked bigger than me. I turned myself into a Bloodhound and gave a low growl.

We hung about outside the train for a long time, just waiting, not doing very much, and after a while the time hung so heavy that I wasn't even sure we'd reach Agra in the twenty-first century. It was characteristic of us to just hang about rather than walk in the same direction as the fat man to determine exactly what had caused the train to halt. The possession of such knowledge would not have made the train move, of course, but it would have allayed my desire for the safe psychological custody of facts which plagued me even in my dreams. But there were no assured facts available. Instead, at regular intervals we heard different stories. Someone said the track had been ripped up by terrorists, someone else said there was definitely a gelignite bomb on the track (his father worked in an arsenal and had taught him to recognize explosives from a distance), a third said the train's engine had collapsed, a fourth said the train driver had collapsed. I contributed my own theory. 'Maybe they've put a speed breaker on the track,' I said cheerfully. 'It's the only place left in India to put one.'

One man grinned, two smiled feebly, and one looked worried. 'Speed breaker?' he asked. 'What are you talking about? How can . . .'

'Airport runways are still left,' said the man who had grinned. I chuckled. The two feeble smilers gave us bemused looks and the worried man's head finally lit up with a tubelight. 'Oh ho,' he said, 'you are joking! Ho ho, that is a very good joke!' He laughed very hard to make up for the delay.

I saw our corpulent foe come triumphantly back from the head of the train. The news he announced chilled us more than all the other rumours. 'There is a dead cow on the track,' he said. 'Some-one has killed it and put it in the way. The driver saw it just in time and pulled the emergency brakes, otherwise there was cent per cent chance the train would have derailed. There is Hindu-Muslim tension in Agra. All trains are being held up. Let us see what happens.'

'How far is Agra?' someone asked.

'Just ten or twelve kilometres,' said his neighbour.

I looked at my watch. It showed 5.30 in the morning. I shud-dered involuntarily and felt a nervous rash of ancient memories jell in that spasm: bayonets held by Chinese soldiers, bayonets seen by Ivan Karamazov when Turkish soldiers tossed infants in the air, two infant brothers in a womb of quilts, the crumbling of walls in Berlin and in my brother's soul.

The opaque haze cleared into a more focussed feeling of being in the inescapable present. The sun would be out in another hour or so. I wondered what we should do. There didn't seem much option except to wait until there was light. After that, if the train didn't move, perhaps we could find some form of road transport into Agra. I was determined to get to the Taj. Inwardly I cursed our months of delay, I cursed the night's dream, I cursed the fat man's authoritative rumour, I cursed the country and its glut of politicians, I cursed the railways and their unexplained delays, I cursed our train with its interminable rows of pissing men and silent women, like Abba I cursed the Union of India. The train stood its ground impassively. My curses floated into the air like tiny parachutes, passing the country by, aimlessly drifting. Nothing changed.

We went back into the bogey and told Mrs Sen what we had learnt. She was philosophical. 'Have some biscuits,' she said, opening a packet. Even Susan opened her mouth to eat one.

Men kept coming in and going out of the compartment. Everyone was fidgety with the delay and the multiple uncertainties of its cause.

'The unidentified object has just been removed,' said a young fellow. 'It was not a bomb.' He had managed to procure himself a cup of tea and a newspaper and looked in possession of the truth.

'So then what *was* it?' I asked.

'Who knows?' he said. 'Maybe cow, maybe pig, maybe some other animal. This is India. Anything is possible. But definitely it was not a bomb, otherwise it could not have been picked up. Now the train is going to start.'

'Are you sure?'

'Definite,' he said, 'I am ninety-nine per cent sure. But this is India. Only God is hundred per cent sure.'

I gave up my futile quest for certainties. I saw myself as a Cocker Spaniel going round and round in chase of my own stump, pursuing inconsequential information to pacify a mindless craving which had worked itself into my hormones and my bones. The only way to overcome it was to remain shut and ask no questions. Like Susan. Or like my brother, for whom words worked as unsatisfactory approximations of the feelings inside him. He said to me once that every time he really wanted to say something, he saw himself come up against words. He only spoke when he could no longer contain the words which built up inside him, and then, when he did, the words came spilling out, as they'd done when he'd been provoked by the fat safari man. For the rest he kept quiet and listened to the 'Emperor' Concerto, which had given sufficient form to all the feelings he ever harboured.

I smiled pleasantly at the man who was drinking tea. Each time he took a sip I felt deprived in my gullet. 'From where did you get the tea?' I asked.

'Outside,' said the fellow helpfully.

I looked outside in all directions. There were neither tea nor newspapers in sight.

'Outside? Where outside?'

'There was a man with a bucket of tea. Maybe he is still there.'

I looked outside, then up and down in case the man with the bucket of tea was hovering above on a parachute, but he had disappeared into thin air. I focussed my mind on solids.

It took another tea-less hour for the train to move: someone said the engine driver had received instructions – presumably from God – to resume the journey only after day broke and the track became more visible. In the compartment it was clear from the hubbub of conversations that there was severe trouble in Agra, and that we'd be lucky to find luggage coolies and transport once we reached the station. We inched forward endlessly. Finally the train stopped at a nearly deserted platform in Agra.

You could pick the news off the tension in the air. We knew instinctively, and this was confirmed by the coolies, that all night there had been riots in the city. Agra was under curfew. The Taj, they told us, was closed to the public until further notice. There were a few coolies asking exorbitant prices to carry luggage. They were immediately hired by the few foreign tourists who had dared the troubled times to make the journey. I felt even sorrier for them than I did for myself: we could come back another time, they might miss their only opportunity to see the Taj.

My brother and I looked at each other. The Taj was closed, there were riots in the city. There was nothing to be said. There was only the immediate problem of somehow finding transport and reaching somewhere safe in that city of great Mughal splendour. There was also Mrs Sen, and silent Susan who had confessed to Mrs Sen that she would be glad of shelter for a day or so. We would have to see them to Mrs Sen's bungalow and take things on from there.

The train, having disgorged its inhabitants, had moved quickly away from the platform, the platform had cleared quicker than I had ever seen, and we found ourselves with two women on a stark road, carrying luggage and still struggling in a direction that might eventually give us a glimpse of the Taj.

We walked a short distance, tense and worried by the absence of life on the streets. The rest of the train's passengers seemed to have made their way somewhere or other, which gave us a little hope. Perhaps we'd find a couple of stray rickshaws, pay them what they wanted, and get to Mrs Sen's house. There didn't seem to be any police in the area, and the few people we had spotted were walking fast.

Then it happened. It happened so quickly that I didn't even register how it happened, or what exactly happened, or why it happened. Its origins, meaning and exact name are unknowable, or at least I do not know them. I only remember the world of the next few moments, when there were no mosques, no caves, no temples, no Scandinavia, no music, no Milan Kundera, only a stone which came hurtling reasonless through the air and hit my brother on his ear, so that he collapsed in a heap. I watched him fall in horror and turned my head, slow motion, in the direction from which the stone had been flung. There was an agony of questions in my jaw muscles. My eyes were wide when something hit me on the head, and as I fell to the ground I saw the Milky Way flash into my blood.

The next day, after I had recovered in Mrs Sen's bungalow, she tried to give me a connected narrative of what had happened. But I think her mind, and Susan's, had both turned into blurs when it happened. According to Mrs Sen three men had emerged from the shadows, examined some of our luggage, picked up some of it, looked about them, and then disappeared. Susan, who seemed to have found her tongue, recalled four men. Perhaps they were poor people taking advantage of an easy target during difficult times, when the cops had taken a respite from the daily grind of elemental nabbing. Or perhaps they were rioters looking for weapons. Or perhaps there was some other story altogether. Mrs Sen was only ninety-nine per cent sure that this is what had happened. Susan was surer. Her percentage was ninety-nine point nine. I didn't trouble them for certainties. Beyond intelligent guesses, there was no way we could be sure of what had happened, nor could the two women who had been technically conscious the whole time. Mrs Sen said all she knew was that she had to transport two half-dead men and one very frightened girl to a bungalow which, she now understood better than ever before, she could not possess for very long.

They managed to cart us to that bungalow somehow. A stray shopkeeper trying surreptitiously to sell his bread and eggs through the curfew saw their plight and emerged; a stray rickshawallah hurrying home knew he had to stop and help. They loaded us on to the rickshaw as best they could. Mrs Sen decided against a hospital; Susan phoned a doctor friend who managed to come to Mrs Sen's, and between him and her own sisterly skills they brought us round.

My injury was comparatively light; the problem was my brother. There was a buzzing sound in his ears and it was obvious that the stone had done some deep internal damage to his hearing. He had to be taken back quickly to ascertain the extent of injury, and though Mrs Sen's extreme hospitality stopped us feeling awkward in her home, a dread of Beethoven's ailment prevented us from staying longer. The next day found us rattling once more to the metronomic clatter of time's winged chariot, hurrying homewards.

From the window of Mrs Sen's guest-room where we had lain recovering, the Taj was visible in the dim distance. Every day, by midday, a haze of dust and traffic pollution rose up into the air and slowly settled over the monument, gradually spreading between the monument and the bungalow. By early afternoon the Taj was lost from sight, and for the rest of the day the only things we could see from the window were branches of gulmohar trees in the lawn below. It was a view which reminded me of a bungalow in which we had once lived. I did not see peacocks come into that garden, as they had done when Mrs Sen was young. Over the two days we were there my brother was too ill and I too anxious to look with any ardour for that bird. Instead, within that haze the images of our life seemed to jell into a surrealist pattern, like a Picasso cow which once formed in the mist. From one side of our gaze there floated down a train of characters, Picasso and Dali, Gorbachev and the Karamazovs, Elizabeth Taylor and Othello, Larkin and Belafonte, a floodlit Nostradamus and the fisherman Hemingway, all led in a slow adagio by the Emperor Beethoven. From the other side, on pretty parachutes, there fell upon us a vaster plumage of peacocks and dwarfs, tigers and hunters, Corbett and hotels, skeletons and rickshaws, the monsoons and the mountains, Shabana Azmi and the Lodi Gardens, all merging in the deep seminal purple of the Pangong Lake.

And we, like puny Nehrus or threadbare Hamlets, thrown there by history, caught by the throat within tidal narratives, tugging and pulling, netting and being netted, having to fathom and connect but wanting only to be alone like a pianist long dead or like slow Sisyphean satellites, out of all reach.

And the Taj? Had it called out to us? Had it anything left to say? Would it stand there for all time as a promise and an appeal, as it had once stood black-and-white for my parents?

I do not think that the Taj called out to us. It did not beckon to us to come, as it had once beckoned my parents. After a few days I stopped thinking of it as music in marble which would play for-ever, waiting to be heard. No, as we lay there feeling desolate, and later from the insecure solitude of our homes, it seemed to stand there only as a neutral monument, black-and-white in the past, visible in full colour at one moment, extinguished by an imper-meable haze at another, solid for a while but eternally vulnerable, an emperor's concerto in stone to which my brother and I, after that unsettling journey through the gathering dark, felt suddenly deaf, immunized by a country, passive as a cow which ate Beetho-ven in the time that Nehru died.